Dare to collect them all!

More books from The Midnight Library:
Nick Shadow's terrifying collection continues . . .

THE MIDNIGHT LIBRARY

LIBRARY

—

Dream Demon

Nick Shadow

*Hodder
Children's
Books*

A division of Hachette Children's Books

Special thanks to Allan Frewin Jones

For John and Joe Noble

'Go team'

Copyright © 2007 Working Partners Limited
Illustrations copyright © 2007 David McDougall
Created by Working Partners Limited, London W6 0QT

First published in Great Britain in 2007
by Hodder Children's Books

1

A Catalogue record for this book is available from the British Library

ISBN-10: 0 340 93025 X
ISBN-13: 978 0 340 93025 0

Typeset in Weiss Antiqua by Avon DataSet Ltd,
Bidford-on-Avon, Warwickshire

The paper a ...
are ...
sustaina ...

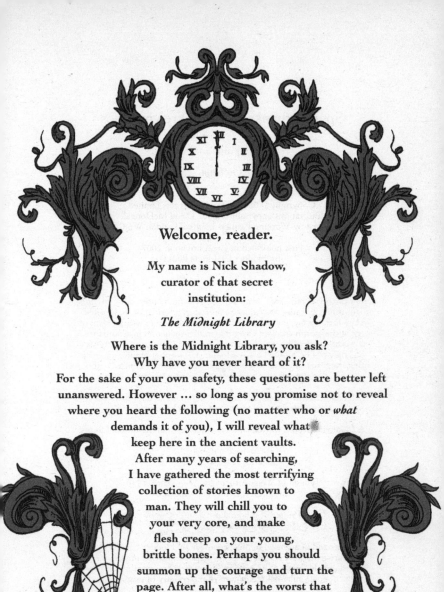

Welcome, reader.

My name is Nick Shadow,
curator of that secret
institution:

The Midnight Library

Where is the Midnight Library, you ask?
Why have you never heard of it?
For the sake of your own safety, these questions are better left
unanswered. However ... so long as you promise not to reveal
where you heard the following (no matter who or *what*
demands it of you), I will reveal what
keep here in the ancient vaults.
After many years of searching,
I have gathered the most terrifying
collection of stories known to
man. They will chill you to
your very core, and make
flesh creep on your young,
brittle bones. Perhaps you should
summon up the courage and turn the
page. After all, what's the worst that
could happen ... ?

The Midnight Library: Volume XI

Stories by Allan Frewin Jones

CONTENTS

DREAM DEMON

Alfie Brennan sat despondently on the edge of the grass, his chin in his hands. Only ten years old and already washed-up as a footballer! At least, that was how he felt after his performance today. OK, so it was only a scratch-team kickabout in the park after school – but that wasn't the point. The point was he had played like a three-legged donkey in a blindfold.

He was the best striker in his year, although you

wouldn't have known it from the way he had been tripping over his feet and mis-kicking right through the match.

A shadow came over him. He looked up gloomily to see Ben Boyd, his best friend, standing over him.

'What's up with you today?' Ben asked. 'You were totally useless out there. Have you got your boots on the wrong feet or something?'

'No,' Alfie said in a way that meant 'shut up and leave me alone'.

Ben frowned. 'You sick?' he asked.

'No.'

'So, what's the problem?'

'Nothing!' Alfie snapped. 'Get lost.'

Instead of getting lost, Ben sat down on the grass verge at Alfie's side. He wrapped his arms around his shins and dropped his chin on to his knees. He didn't say anything, he just sat there beside Alfie, staring out across the park and whistling softly.

After a minute of two, Alfie glanced at him. 'My mum's got a new job,' Alfie said.

'Right . . .' Ben murmured, and stopped whistling.

'I'm really pleased she's got the job,' Alfie continued, 'because she's been out of work for ages, but she's got to go on this initiation course before she can start. It's up in Birmingham and it's going to last for the whole weekend. *This* weekend. It means she'll be away Friday and Saturday night and I've got to go and stay with my gran, and she doesn't have cable or satellite or anything! And even worse, her TV is so incredibly ancient that I can't even plug my PlayStation into it.'

'So ask your mum to take *your* TV over there,' Ben suggested.

'I did, but she said it was hardly worth it just for two days. So I said, yes it really, *really* was worth it, and she said, "Well you'll just have to do without it 'cos there's no way we're going to be able to get the widescreen TV in my little car." And then she told

3

me not to moan because she had "other things to think about".' He gave a deep sigh. 'That's why I played so badly today. I've got a whole weekend with no TV and no PlayStation to look forward to and it's doing my head in.' He glanced at Ben, who looked sympathetic. 'Plus,' Alfie added, a bit embarrassed to make his next confession. 'Plus, I'm going to be sleeping in a room where someone died!'

Alfie was about to add 'and that totally creeps me out', when Ben's eyes widened and a grin spread across his face.

'No way!' Ben breathed.

Alfie nodded solemnly.

'That's so cool! Is there a ghost and stuff?' Ben demanded.

Alfie gave him a long, thoughtful look. He hadn't considered it this way before. Maybe it was cool . . . 'I don't think there's a ghost,' he said cautiously. 'At least, nobody's ever mentioned one.'

'So, who died?' Ben asked eagerly.

'My mum's brother,' Alfie said.

'Was he murdered or something?' Ben asked with ghoulish relish.

'No, he wasn't *murdered!*' Alfie said, frowning. 'He just died. He was the same age as me. His mum – my gran – went up to his room one morning to wake him up for school and he'd died in the night.'

'Wow! What did he die of?'

'Dunno,' Alfie said. 'Mum was only four years old at the time, and Gran never told her. All she knows is she had an older brother called Martin who died in bed one night. He wasn't ill or anything – he just died. My gran doesn't like talking about it.'

'No, I don't suppose she would,' Ben said thoughtfully. He looked eagerly at Alfie. 'Are you going to be sleeping in the same bed he died in?'

'*No!*' Alfie almost yelled. 'My mum wouldn't make me sleep in a bed where someone died! What kind of sicko are you?' He got up. 'I'm going home. See you tomorrow.'

He stomped off, as Ben made ghostly *whooo-ooo-ooo* noises behind him.

* * *

'Uh, Mum?' Alfie asked cautiously as she drove their old Volkswagen Beetle towards his gran's house after school the following day. 'Has Granny Dorry bought a new bed for the room I'll be sleeping in?'

She frowned. 'I don't think so,' she replied. 'Why?'

He swallowed hard. This had been on his mind ever since that freakazoid, Ben, had first mentioned it. 'I don't want to sleep in the bed where Uncle Martin died,' he said with a shudder.

His mother laughed. 'Oh, for heaven's sake, is that what's been on your mind? I knew there was something. Listen, Alfie, sweetheart, that room has been totally redecorated. Even the furniture is different now from how it was back then.' She glanced at him. 'Listen, that all happened a long time ago – thirty years ago. And it was a *sad* thing to happen, not a *creepy* thing. Do you get the difference?'

'Um, ye-es, of course,' Alfie said. Sad was when someone young died unexpectedly. Creepy was when they came back as a vampire ghost and sucked your brains out through your eye sockets, he thought. Alfie got the difference – he hoped dead Uncle Martin did too!

'And please don't start asking your gran lots of questions about it either,' his mother continued. 'It was a terrible tragedy for her, and she doesn't like to be reminded of it.'

'I won't,' Alfie said. He was relieved just to have found out that it wasn't the same bed. He stared out of the window as they drove around the huge, derelict industrial estate that sprawled between the town where he lived with his mum and his gran's lonely cottage on the edge of the open countryside.

If you could cut straight through the industrial estate, it was only about a kilometre from his house to his gran's, but the abandoned factory complex was so huge that the road looped for almost four kilometres to get around it.

Alfie stared at the tall factory buildings, with their broken windows, surrounded by dumped cars and courtyards sprouting grass. A few years ago he and Ben had played in there all the time, but then signs had been put up saying 'KEEP OUT! DANGER OF FALLING MASONRY', and his mum had made him promise not to go in there any more.

Once past the industrial estate, the car slowly wound its way up the road that climbed the wooded hillside. At the crest, Alfie knew what they would see: a great wrinkled stretch of farms and woods stretching away into the hazy blue distance, and, just under the long downward slope of the hill, the ruined old abbey standing right next to his gran's solitary cottage.

'Come on, old girl,' his mum urged as the car approached the top of the hill. 'You can do it.' She flashed Alfie a look. 'I don't think we'd have made it with the TV on board, do you?'

'Probably not,' Alfie admitted.

'You'll be OK without it over the weekend, won't you?' she said. 'You and Granny Dorry will find loads of things to do.'

He smiled at her. He knew that she was worried about the course and he didn't want to make things harder for her by admitting that he expected this to be the most tedious weekend of his entire life. 'Of course we will,' he said. 'Who needs TV?'

They both chorused, '*We* do!' and then laughed as the car came over the top of the hill and gathered speed on the downward slope.

'Almost there,' his mum said. 'Can you see the cottage yet?'

Alfie peered through the windscreen. There were a lot of trees in the way. He could see the grey stone walls of the ruined medieval abbey poking above the trees. His gran's cottage was just behind it. 'No, not yet,' he replied.

In winter the tall cottage chimney could be seen from here, but in summer it was hidden by leafy treetops. They came down the hill and drove past the abbey. It was set back from the road, behind a wide, grassy churchyard dotted with crumbling old tombs and mossy headstones that leaned at strange angles. Alfie remembered Granny Dorry saying that the churchyard dated from the eighteenth century and hadn't been used for a long time now.

Alfie's mum drove the car around a final bend, and there was the cottage straight ahead of them. It nestled behind a big front garden full of rambling rose bushes, cherry trees and overgrown flower-beds. It was warm and friendly and welcoming – a lot like Granny Dorry herself, in fact.

His mum parked the car and they headed in through the rustic arched gateway, pushing past dangling passion flowers and stepping over the larger of the plants that had shoved their way up between the paving stones. Alfie had his holdall over his shoulder. It contained his pyjamas, a couple of changes of clothes and a few books and magazines to help him pass the time.

And there was Granny Dorry, standing smiling under the wooden porch with her arms out.

Alfie ran up and hugged her. 'Hello, Gran!' he said happily. She smelled of baking mixed in with beeswax furniture polish.

'I heard the car,' she said. 'How are you both? Isn't it exciting about your new job, Suzanna? I hope you're not going to be too bored, Alfie, without all those television channels you're used to. But come on in. I've just taken some chocolate muffins out of the oven and we can have a nice cup of tea.'

They crowded into the small hallway and made their way through into the large kitchen. The windows looked out over the abbey. Sometimes Alfie thought the ruin looked a bit eerie, but in the bright sunshine the crumbling walls were really quite picturesque. Granny Dorry obviously thought so too, judging by the number of watercolour paintings of the abbey lining the walls of the cottage.

Painting watercolours was his gran's favourite hobby – she even painted birthday cards and Christmas cards every year. Alfie thought she was very good. When he was younger, she had shown him some painting techniques. He'd enjoyed it at the time, but then football and PlayStation had taken over and he'd pretty much given up on paints and brushes.

'Go and put your things up in your room,' Granny Dorry told Alfie. 'It's all aired out and fresh for you.'

Alfie left his gran and his mum chatting in the kitchen. The top floor of the cottage was reached by climbing a narrow, twisty staircase. The uneven white walls were dotted with more of Granny Dorry's watercolours.

Alfie knew the room he would be sleeping in. First door on the left. It had been painted leaf-green since last he'd been here. He hesitated for a moment outside the closed door. What if he opened the door and saw . . . *something*?

He took a deep breath, turned the handle and gave the door a hefty push. The room had been painted a light, creamy yellow and there were several of his gran's paintings on the walls. The window was open and the whole place was full of sunlight and fresh summer air. Alfie walked in and dumped his holdall on the bed. Then he ran back downstairs. The cheery look of the room had banished all thoughts of ghosts from his mind. He felt that the only thing he had to worry about over the next couple of days was how to avoid going crazy with boredom.

Alfie's mum stayed for about half an hour. The three of them sat in the kitchen eating muffins while Alfie's mum gave his gran an update on everything he was doing at school.

After his mum had driven off, Granny Dorry took Alfie on a tour of the wild back garden and showed him what she called her 'bird restaurant', where she had containers of seeds and peanuts and fat-balls and a birdbath for the wild birds.

'You can help me refill the containers, if you like,' she told him, her arm around his shoulders. 'And I have a pair of binoculars so you could do some bird-spotting. I'll show you my bird book. You'll be able to look up any bird you don't recognize.'

Alfie's heart sank. Two days of bird-watching? That was it – this was now officially the worst weekend of his life.

'Would you like that?' Gran asked.

'You bet,' Alfie said with a smile. He loved his gran loads and the last thing he wanted to do was upset her by telling her what he really thought of bird-watching.

'And we could do some painting together,' Gran suggested. 'How does that sound?'

'Cool,' Alfie said, secretly thinking he deserved an Oscar for his performance.

'Tell you what,' Gran said. 'How about I make us something to eat, and then I'll get out all the family photo albums. Remember how you used to like it when I showed you all those old pictures?'

In his mind, Alfie dropped down dead on the grass. Wonderful as Granny Dorry was, she seemed to have forgotten that he'd *grown up* a whole lot since those days. 'Yes, I remember,' he said, desperately hoping, as they walked back to the garden door of the cottage, that she'd have forgotten about the albums by the time they'd had dinner.

For probably the first time in his life, barring Christmas Eve, Alfie was quite glad when it came to bedtime. An evening of pretending to be interested in old family photos had worn him out. Not that the old albums had been the only entertainment on offer. Not at all. Granny Dorry also had a whole cabinet full of ancient jigsaw puzzles with missing pieces and weird old board games with no instructions, and she'd even found a deck of Happy Families cards where a lot of the families seemed to have split up and the kids left home!

Up in his room, Alfie walked over to the window to draw the curtains. He was intrigued by how different the view was by moonlight. The moon was full, hanging low in the sky right above the old abbey. The shimmery white light made the broken walls look unreal, as if they might dissolve into pale shreds of mist and go floating away over the treetops at any moment.

A shiver ran up Alfie's back. He could see the oddly angled gravestones in the churchyard, and the neglected tombs. They looked rather spooky, standing there in pools of black shadow. Alfie quickly drew the curtains closed.

He switched on the bedside light, got into his pyjamas and slid between the cool sheets. *One evening down*, he thought. *Only one more to go*. And maybe during the day tomorrow he could go exploring.

He began to doze off.

The ringing of deep, sonorous bells woke him up. He had no idea how much time had passed. A couple of minutes? A few hours? Alfie lay in bed with his eyes closed, listening to the distant booming of the bells. *Clang! Clang! Clang!*

'Of course, it's the abbey,' he murmured to himself. 'Don't those monks ever sleep?' He turned over, pulling the blankets up over his head.

Hey, wait a minute, he thought drowsily, *the abbey is just a load of ruins. It doesn't even* have *a bell-tower any more . . .*

But moments later he was asleep again, and the bells were just a remote echo in the back of his mind.

The next thing he knew, Alfie was standing in the old churchyard, staring at the ruined abbey — except that it wasn't in ruins any more. It towered up above him, solid and complete with a high, pointed roof and soaring towers, its stone walls shining in the odd golden-brown light of the setting sun. The strange light that the ochre sun cast across the countryside was reflected in the glass of the tall abbey windows. At one end of the huge building, a big round window faced the fading sun, glittering with light like a fly's eye.

Alfie gazed around himself. There were gravestones still, but far fewer, and they were all standing upright, tanned pale brown by the creeping twilight and throwing immensely long shadows.

A slow breeze drifted past him, filling his head with the smell of wet grass. He realized it must have rained recently, and looking down at the grass, he saw that it was spangled with water droplets. The air was heavy with moisture too, making it damp and sticky and hard to breathe.

The clamour of bells rang in his ears, hanging in the air like storm clouds.

Oh, yes, like before, Alfie thought. *They woke me up. I remember*. He looked over his shoulder. Granny Dorry's cottage should have been there, twenty metres or so behind him, but it wasn't. There were just fields and woods. No other buildings at all. He felt a pang of unease – how was he going to get back home? But then it struck him that he must be dreaming.

Hey, what's the problem? he asked himself. *This isn't real. It's a dream, and it's the most realistic dream I've ever had! I'd better make the most of it before I wake up.*

He walked towards the looming abbey, noticing for the first time that there were lights behind some of the tall windows. Flickering lights. Candles.

There must be someone inside, he thought.

He came out of the rain-slick grass and walked along a wide gravel path. He noticed blades of grass sticking to his shoes, and saw that the bottoms of his jeans were dark with water. He glanced back. The sun was almost gone now. It would soon be night.

Alfie walked up to the large oak doors of the abbey. The solid wooden panels were studded with black iron bolts. And there were two black iron rings for handles. There didn't seem to be a bell or a knocker.

He was just reaching for one of the iron handles when the bells stopped ringing. The sudden silence was quite startling. He shivered as he glanced over his shoulder. The sun was gone and the golden-brown light had faded from the sky. Where previously the churchyard and the surrounding fields had been striped by light and shade, all was now sunk in darkness.

Alfie had the distinct feeling that it would be friendlier inside. He grasped the big black ring with both hands and turned it. He was aware of creakings and clunkings from close behind the doors, as though some great big, old mechanism was moving slowly and ponderously. He pushed cautiously at the door and it swung open without a sound. Then he peeped in through the gap, just in case the place was full of people, but he couldn't see anybody.

Cautiously, Alfie stepped over the stone

threshold and into the abbey. The great church opened up in front of him, lit by scores and scores of candles. By their light, he could see that the smooth white walls soared up to a high vaulted ceiling of carved stone. A line of stone pillars stretched along the central aisle, and on either side of the aisle were rows and rows of wooden pews. At the far end was a raised platform with an altar on it, over which a white cloth was spread.

Fascinated by the silent beauty of the magnificent abbey, Alfie walked slowly down the aisle. He was almost at the altar when a movement in the shadows off to the left caught the corner of his eye. He turned, catching his breath. He wasn't alone after all.

A grey shape stood, half concealed, behind a fluted pillar, a figure wearing what looked like a medieval monk's habit: a long grey robe with a deep hood. A shiver ran down Alfie's spine as he stared at the figure. The man was turned away from him, as though he was concentrating on the altar and hadn't realized Alfie was there.

Alfie swallowed hard, trying to stay calm. He was in a church, and the man was obviously a monk; there was nothing to be scared of. He gave a small cough.

The figure turned slowly to face him, and Alfie felt a thrill of utter terror. As the monk's hood turned in his direction, he found himself staring into nothing. There was no face at all, just a well of darkness like a hole in the world. Alfie felt giddy as he looked into that empty void. It wasn't the darkness of deep shadow, it was a darkness like the night sky – a darkness that could suck you in and leave you tumbling for ever and ever through space.

The monk took a step towards Alfie and Alfie backed away, feeling an overwhelming sensation of danger and menace. Although his eyes were fixed on the terrifying emptiness within the hood, Alfie was aware of the monk untying the rope belt from around his waist and twisting the rope-ends around his white, skeletal-thin hands, stretching it tight as he advanced.

Using all his willpower, Alfie wrenched his gaze away from the approaching figure and ran for the doors. Everything else was forgotten in his panic to get out of the abbey.

The door he had entered through had swung shut. A voice in his head said, *You'll never get it open again in time.* 'Yes I will . . .' Alfie snarled as he raced for the doors. He couldn't hear anything behind him, but he didn't dare look back. It had been difficult to tear his eyes away from the darkness under the hood. He didn't have the courage to look into it again.

With a gasp of relief, he reached the doors, grabbed the black ring with both hands and hauled on it. The door didn't move. Alfie cried in frustration and pulled on the ring with all his strength, but it was hopeless. Glancing frantically over his shoulder, Alfie saw the monk move up the aisle towards him, the rope still held taut between his hands. But the monk was walking slowly, almost as if he knew the doors would be locked, as if he knew there was no way for Alfie to get out.

Alfie stared around the church, searching for another exit. To his right he saw a second pair of arched double doors. 'Yes!' Alfie exclaimed, darting behind the back row of pews towards them. He could see that one of the doors was slightly ajar. Alfie rammed into it, shoulder first, pushing it further open and stumbling through the gap. He turned, slammed the door shut behind him and leaned against it, trying to catch his breath, and stared into the gloom ahead.

A narrow stone corridor stretched into the shadows. On one side, pillared arches opened on to a paved courtyard, and Alfie thought he could see another door at the far end of the shadowy cloister. Should he run for that distant door, or stay where he was and hold *this* door closed against the thing in the hooded robe?

He ran. Echoes of his footfalls filled his ears,

drowning out any sound of pursuit. When he reached the door, Alfie lifted the latch and pushed it open eagerly. He slipped through, finally risking a glance over his shoulder as he went. He gave a yelp of fear and surprise. The grey monk was only a couple of metres behind him, silent and deadly with the rope held out tight at neck height. But the monk was still moving at a walking pace, so how could he be so *close*? Alfie slammed the door in what would have been the monk's face – if he'd had one.

He had to get out of the abbey, but the place seemed huge! He took a deep breath and began to run again. Alfie glanced behind him. Though he hadn't heard the door open, the hooded figure was still following him, slowly, steadily, unerringly.

Alfie ran up a flight of stone stairs, through another badly lit room, down another corridor. There were windows – he could see down into the churchyard below – but they didn't open. He raced on, through another room, along another narrow passage, down a staircase that led to a long thin room filled with tables and chairs. Alfie was beginning to feel like a rat in a maze, running and running with no hope of ever finding the way out.

In a final desperate effort to throw the grey monk off his trail, Alfie ducked under one of the tables and crawled into a dark corner to hide. Then he peeped out to keep an eye on the foot of the stairway.

A few moments later the monk reached the foot of the stairs and walked into the room, his long robes sweeping the floor. For a moment he paused, as if he wasn't sure where Alfie had gone. But the next moment, he walked unerringly towards Alfie's hiding-place.

Alfie stifled a groan, praying that his pursuer didn't know he was there. The monk threw chairs aside as he drew closer, and then the table above Alfie shifted. With a yell of terror, Alfie scrambled out of his hiding-place. The monk lunged forward and tried to loop the rope around his neck.

Alfie ducked and the rope missed by a fraction. Now he understood what the rope was for – the monk seemed intent on using it to strangle him. Alfie vaulted another table and ran to another door at the far end of the room. He threw it open and found himself back in the cloistered courtyard. He groaned with frustration – so much running and he was almost back where he had started. But there was no time to think about that. The grey monk was crossing the room towards him, so Alfie ran for the church; there was nowhere else for him to go.

He hauled the church door open and stumbled inside. The monk was so close behind him now that he didn't even have time to close the door. He just ran on, frantically looking for another way out.

He could see only the main doors where he had first come in, and he already knew that they were locked, but then he glimpsed a small doorway set into the stone wall on the far side of the huge room.

He sprinted for it, ignoring the painful stitch beginning to bite into his side, and lifted the latch. The door opened into deep gloom. Alfie stepped over the threshold, and almost fell down the stone staircase that began right at his feet. He swung over the empty darkness for a moment before he regained his balance, then slammed the door shut behind him and descended the stairs.

Now that he was in almost complete darkness, Alfie could see a small yellow light wavering far below him. He knew enough about churches to have a nasty feeling that the stairs were leading him to the crypt. Still, he had no choice, so he continued towards the light and finally found himself emerging from the stairway across a wide stone floor.

The flickering yellow light turned out to be from a few thick candles that stood in stone bowls around the walls. The room smelled of damp and decay, of mouldy earth and the sweet, sickly stench of rotting wood. The candle flames guttered and leaped, sending dark shadows racing over the dank stone walls. Pale roots and tendrils of ivy dangled from the low ceiling, brushing horribly against Alfie's face as he made his way across the room. He had been right about the crypt. Great heavy stone tombs reared up around him, and the walls were lined with deep, oblong holes housing ancient coffins.

There was no sign of the monk. Alfie held his breath, listening for the evil creature's approach, but his pulse was hammering in his head and he couldn't hear a thing. Suddenly a deadly realization hit him: there was no way out of the subterranean chamber, no way other than to head back up the stairs down which he'd come, the stairs down which the monk was probably already making his slow, certain way. Alfie was trapped.

And even while he was coming to terms with that terrible thought, a dark shadow moved at the bottom of the stairs. *Perhaps this has been his plan all along*, Alfie thought, *to chase and chase me until I got cornered in a place with no way out.*

But he could still hide, he realized. He ran deeper into the shadows of the crypt, ducking behind the massive tombs, searching for a hiding-place.

Eventually, he crouched in a gloomy corner, trying to catch his breath, staring out around the corner of crumbling stonework, watching for the monk.

A breath of cold air touched the back of Alfie's neck, and he shivered. The monk was moving slowly through the crypt now. Maybe, if he circled around, he could get behind the monk and make a dash for the stairs. Anything would be better than just sitting there waiting for the feel of that rope around his neck.

Another breath of air ruffled his hair, and suddenly its significance hit him. He looked over his shoulder. He was close to the back wall of the crypt, and above him, where the slimy walls met the vaulted ceiling, he saw a narrow strip of darkness that was different to the shadowy gloom of the rest of the crypt.

Alfie stared at that patch of darkness and suddenly realized that he was looking at the night sky, showing through a rift in the stonework. Some rubble on top of the tomb behind him indicated that part of the ceiling had caved in.

Here was a way out.

Alfie leaped up, scrambling on to the flat top of the tomb, climbing over the rubble to reach up to the hole in the ceiling. Cold air was blowing right in his face now, and to Alfie it meant freedom.

He gripped the rough stone edges and hauled himself upwards, his feet scrabbling for purchase on the walls. Soon his head and shoulders were through the hole and he could smell wet grass and feel earth beneath his fingers. Panting with exertion and almost crying with relief,

Alfie squirmed and wriggled his way up into the churchyard.

One final foothold to push himself up and he'd be out. But then he felt something cold grasp his ankle – a hand so icy that a bone-deep chill spread quickly up his leg, deadening his senses, filling him with despair.

With his last ounce of energy and determination, Alfie kicked out. The grip loosened for an instant and he was able to drag his trailing leg up through the hole. He went rolling across the wet grass, shivering with coldness and fear.

He scrambled to his feet, but his leg was still numb. He had to hobble along, dragging his leg, but at least he was out of that dreadful abbey, and away from the evil grey monk.

As he stumbled across the churchyard, Alfie glanced back nervously and, in that instant, all hope left him, for the monk was climbing effortlessly up out of the crypt, his grey hood still framing a void of horrifying blackness.

A sudden intense pain in his leg brought Alfie to a jarring halt. He had crashed into one of the gravestones, opening a gash in his knee. He staggered sideways and fell, hitting his head on another stone.

He was vaguely aware of dancing red flames at the edges of his vision, of the gravestones towering over him as he lay on his back in the grass. And then a fierce chill flooded through him and Alfie felt as if he was falling for ever into a bottomless black abyss.

Alfie woke with a start, trembling and sweating. He forced his eyes open. He was lying in bed and a pale light was trickling in around the curtains of his room. He could hear birds singing loudly outside his window.

With a huge rush of relief, he realized that he was in bed at Granny Dorry's house. He threw the sheets and blankets back and sat up on the edge of the bed.

'Talk about bad dreams!' he breathed, rubbing his eyes. But the nightmare had been so real! He'd never had a dream like it before. 'And hopefully I never will again,' he muttered to himself, standing up to go and pull the curtains.

'Ow!' Alfie felt a sharp pain in his right leg, and he sat down again, nursing his knee in both hands. The dream was still uncomfortably vivid in his mind, and this was the same knee that he had injured in the churchyard.

Puzzled, he rolled up his pyjama leg. There was a bit of swelling on the side of his knee, and a dark bruise was beginning to appear under the skin. Alfie stared at it in total confusion. How had he done that?

He looked thoughtfully at the corner of the bedside table. If he'd been kicking and struggling in his nightmare, Alfie supposed he could easily have banged his knee against it. In fact, banging his knee in real life was probably what had made him dream of crashing into a gravestone. He'd heard of things like that before, where real things – like someone calling your name or a telephone ringing – found their way into a dream.

He stood up, and walked over to the window. The pain in his knee wasn't so bad – it just felt a bit awkward and stiff. He opened the curtains and gazed out over Granny Dorry's garden to the ruined abbey.

That had been one mad, freakish dream! Alfie thought. But then, sleeping in a strange bed, in a room where someone had died, and with the ruined abbey only a stone's throw away, it was hardly surprising that he'd had a weird dream.

He heard the radio playing downstairs. Granny Dorry must be up. He looked at his bedside clock. It was half past seven. Alfie decided he might as well get up now too – especially as he thought he could smell bacon frying.

He grinned to himself as he crossed the landing to the bathroom. Mad invisible monks with strangling ropes! His dream would have made a pretty good scary movie – except that he'd ruined the grisly end by waking up too soon. But he wasn't sorry about that. He didn't particularly like the idea of getting strangled – not even in a dream!

The sun was shining brightly down out of a clear blue sky as Alfie and his gran sat eating breakfast on her patio.

'Well, then,' Granny Dorry said, smiling at Alfie over her teacup. 'What shall we do today? It's far too nice to be indoors. Do you still like to paint, Alfie?'

'I don't do it so much these days,' he admitted.

'That's a shame. You were very good at it. I still have a few of your paintings, you know. There's one in particular that I like. It's of a leaf – just the one leaf – and it fills the entire page. You painted in every single vein. It's a lovely piece of work.'

'Yes, I remember that,' Alfie said. 'I spent hours on it.' He smiled. 'It was fun, actually.'

'Tell you what,' said Granny Dorry, putting

her teacup down. 'How about I pack us a nice picnic and we go and do some painting together? I've got enough paper, paints and brushes for both of us.'

Alfie grinned at his gran. 'Yes, why not?' he said. 'That's a great idea.' And he really meant it. He hadn't picked up a paint-brush for three or four years, and he was curious to see how his painting would turn out.

'We needn't go very far to find ourselves a good subject,' Granny Dorry pointed out. 'We can start off with a few pictures of the old abbey. What do you say?'

Alfie glanced across at the abbey. It looked a whole lot less spooky in the bright sunshine than it had in his nightmare. 'Sounds good to me,' he agreed. 'Is there any more bacon?'

'I think I can rustle up another slice or two, especially if we're going to have a hard morning's painting ahead of us,' his gran replied with a smile.

Alfie grinned as his gran headed in through the garden door. He was looking forward to painting. Maybe this wasn't going to be such a boring weekend after all.

Alfie and his gran were sitting on small fold-out canvas stools in the churchyard on the far side of the abbey. They each had a portable easel for their pads of cartridge paper, and a small table stood between them, holding their paints and water bowls. Just behind them, a wicker picnic basket sat in the grass.

Alfie had already finished the foreground of his picture. He had painted in the white abbey walls, now he wanted to add some sky. He dabbed his brush in the cerulean blue that he had just squeezed from the tube. Straight away, he could see that the colour would be too strong, so he squeezed out some white and mixed the two together until he had the shade he wanted.

He stared at the abbey again. This time

something odd struck him as he looked at the empty arch of an old doorway. Wasn't this more or less the place where he had found himself at the start of his dream? He stared at the walls and towers, trying to imagine how they would have looked before they had fallen into ruin. Yes, this *was* the place, he felt sure. No wonder he hadn't been able to see Granny Dorry's cottage behind him – he had been looking in the wrong place. The cottage would have been over the other side of the abbey.

He imagined the grey monk standing in the doorway, and grinned to himself. *Sorry, mister*, he thought, *you're just not scary any more.*

But even as those words entered his head, a shadow came sweeping across the abbey, turning the white stones to a dull leaden grey, and taking all the brightness out of the landscape.

'Uh-oh!' Alfie heard his gran say. 'Some clouds are moving in. I think it's going to rain.'

Alfie looked up into the sky. Heavy grey clouds

had covered the sun, and in the distant west, the sky was dark with rain.

'Let's finish our picnic while it's still dry out here and then we'll head back to the cottage,' Granny Dorry suggested.

Alfie nodded and searched in the hamper for his sandwich.

'Do you remember the ghost stories I used to tell you about the old abbey?' Granny Dorry asked as they ate.

Alfie shook his head, his mouth full of food. 'Not really,' he mumbled.

'You don't remember about the ghost monk?'

Alfie nearly choked on his sandwich. He swallowed hard, his eyes watering as he forced the food down. 'What ghost monk?' he coughed, banging his chest with the flat of his hand.

'Oh, you used to love the story about the spooky old monk who haunted the ruins of the abbey on the nights of the full moon,' Granny Dorry told him.

A faint memory slid into Alfie's mind. He could vaguely remember, years ago, sitting on the carpet in front of the log fire in Granny Dorry's living-room, gazing up at her, spellbound, as she sat in her big armchair. She had told him spooky stories and, yes, now he came to think about it, one had been about the abbey and *the ghost monk in the grey robes*!

So that was where the nightmare had come from, Alfie realized. His gran's story must have got itself locked away in his subconscious, and it had suddenly popped up as a weird, scary dream! It was actually kind of cool.

Alfie grinned, feeling hugely relieved. 'Yes, I remember!' he exclaimed. 'He'd wander about with his arms stretched out, and you couldn't see his face under his hood!'

'That's right,' Granny Dorry said with a smile. 'And I used to have to give you a big hug afterwards and tell you it was only make-believe.'

Alfie looked at her. 'Not really necessary now, Gran, thanks,' he said.

'You're never too old for a hug, Alfie,' she laughed. 'You were quite young then, so I never told you the really spooky part about the monk,' she went on. 'Would you like to hear the full story now? I think you're old enough.'

'You bet,' he said, still feeling happy to have discovered that his dream was just part of an old story he'd forgotten he'd even heard. He was quite keen to hear the full story now.

'Well, legend has it that the hooded monk was once a notorious executioner. This was back in the fifteenth century when the abbey was still in one piece. But eventually he was condemned to death himself. He was found guilty of treason, and in those days people were executed in particularly nasty ways if they had committed treason. They nailed him into a coffin and buried him alive, and that's why his spirit can never rest.' Granny Dorry nodded thoughtfully. 'I dare say it served him right,' she said. 'He had an especially unpleasant way of executing his victims. He used to garrotte them.'

Alfie frowned at her. 'What does that mean?'

'He used to strangle them with a hank of rope,' his gran explained. And at the same moment, large drops of rain began to fall around them. 'Oh, bother! It's started raining,' Granny Dorry said. 'Quicksticks, Alfie! Let's get everything back to the cottage before it gets soaked.'

They managed to rush everything into the cottage before the rain really began to pelt down. They laid their paintings out on the kitchen table and Granny Dorry put a pan of milk on the stove to make them both some hot chocolate.

'That was a close-run thing,' she said. 'Look at it out there, it's raining cats and dogs!'

Alfie *was* looking. He was standing at the kitchen window and staring out through the falling sheets of rain to where the upper parts of the abbey walls could be seen above the trees at the bottom of the garden. The abbey looked grey and sombre under the miserable sky, but it was not the sight of the grim walls that was preoccupying Alfie. It was the fact that in his dream, the ghost monk had come at him with a thick length of rope stretched between his hands, as if he was going to strangle him with it. *But if Granny Dorry never told me that part of the story, how did I know about it to put it in my dream?* Alfie wondered.

I must have heard about it somehow, he thought. *Maybe I read it in a book of local legends, or, more likely, Granny Dorry did tell me that part of the story, and then she just forgot.*

'The hot chocolate's ready,' his gran said, breaking into his thoughts. 'Tell you what, let's take it through into the living-room and we can look at our pictures while we drink it.'

Alfie carried the paintings into the living-room and propped them up on chairs. Then he and his gran sat down on the sofa with their hot chocolate to look at them.

Granny Dorry had completed two pictures — both done in an enviable flowing style that made the abbey and the countryside behind it seem to come alive on the paper. By comparison, Alfie thought his sole effort looked a little awkward, but it was vivid and detailed.

'I really like it,' his gran said, looking closely at Alfie's picture. 'You've caught the feel of the old place, you really have: all gaunt and spectral.' She glanced at him. 'Are you sure you haven't done any painting recently?'

'None at all,' Alfie said. He looked at his picture again. Maybe it wasn't so bad.

'Oh, that's a shame, though,' his gran went on. She pointed to a dark grey smear under the arch of the entrance in the painting. 'The rain's made a smudge.'

Alfie looked more closely. Sure enough, there was a grey mark in the arched doorway, but to Alfie's eyes, it didn't look like a stain caused by a raindrop, it looked like the small hooded figure of a grey-robed monk.

* * *

Alfie had difficulty getting to sleep that night. He knew it was only in his imagination, but he didn't like the idea of another night spent fleeing in panic from the ghost monk. Once was enough, thanks very much. And it didn't help that his gran had brought his painting up to his room and propped it up on his bedside table.

He lay in the darkness, deliberately facing away from the painting, but it still felt to him as if that weird, smudgy figure was staring at him from under the doorway. It gave him a really uncomfortable feeling between his shoulder blades.

He tried to take his mind off it. He imagined how his pal Ben would laugh if he ever found out that Alfie had been too scared of bad dreams to go to sleep. The image of Ben yelling with laughter did the trick. The ghost monk faded from his mind and Alfie drifted off to sleep.

He found himself lying in the churchyard under the night sky. The grass was wet beneath him and there was a sharp pain in his right knee. He lifted his head with a groan. 'Oh, no!' The dark gravestones towered around him and he could hear a stealthy, slithery kind of sound behind him.

He levered himself up and stared over his shoulder. The ghost monk was gliding towards him over the dank grass, the rope glistening slightly as he held it tight between his thin hands.

Alfie scrabbled to his feet, his shoes slipping on the wet grass as he ran. His first instinct was to get as far away from the horrible abbey as possible. He made a dash for the wooded hills, but the evil grey shape of the monk, now suddenly in front of him, came floating silently across his path. Alfie came to a sliding halt, almost falling in his attempt to change direction quickly. He dodged in and out of the gravestones, running at full pelt. But the monk was ahead of him again, and so it continued. No matter how hard Alfie ran, no matter which direction he took, the monk was always right there in front of him, a menacing, faceless figure with a rope stretched between his hands.

The only route left led directly back to the abbey. The big oak doors of the church were open this time, almost as if they had been left open deliberately to entice him inside. He had no choice. He raced into the candlelit church, pausing only to snatch hold of the doors and swing them closed.

As he shut out the grim night, he saw the monk coming towards him, but the doors slammed together with a reassuring thud. This time, Alfie noticed a wooden bar on a pivot that could be brought down to hold the doors shut.

He jumped up and grabbed the solid oak bar with both hands, bringing it down with a crash into its two iron cradles. He staggered back, panting. The doors were locked now. The monk couldn't get at him – unless he could pass right through solid oak.

The noise of heavy blows resounded through the

church, and Alfie saw the doors shudder. The monk was beating on them, trying to get in. Then the hammering stopped to be replaced by scraping, scratching noises that set Alfie's teeth on edge. It sounded as if the monk was clawing at the doors like a rat, trying to rip his way through them with his fingernails.

Alfie let out a wild laugh. 'Scratch all you like, mister!' he yelled. 'No way are you getting in here!' He backed away from the doors, breathing hard. Then he remembered the double doors that led to the cloister. He ran over to them and slammed a heavy iron bolt home, locking them securely. He ran back to the main doors. The unpleasant scratching sound had stopped now. Alfie's eyes narrowed. *That was too easy. How come the monk's given up so quickly?* he wondered. *Maybe there's another way into the church . . .*

And, with that, Alfie suddenly remembered the crypt – and the long narrow split in the stonework through which he'd made his escape last time. He could still see in his mind the way the ghost had glided up out of that hole. The monk could get in just as easily. Alfie spun around, staring over at the small door that led down to the crypt.

It stood ajar. Moaning with renewed fear, he ran for the door and dragged it closed with a hollow bang. But there was no lock – no way of keeping it closed against the monk. Alfie stared around in desperation. What could he use to block the door? He looked at the pews. They seemed heavy enough. If he could just drag a few of them over and pile them up in the doorway, Alfie thought it might be enough to keep the monk out.

He ran over and grabbed hold of the back of one of the pews. He dug his heels in and pulled. His fingers ached. Sweat ran down his face. The heavy pew moved a few centimetres, the wood grating on the stone tiles of the floor.

Alfie gritted his teeth and pulled again with all his strength. The pew scraped another few centimetres across the floor.

He felt a chill air on the back of his neck, and twisted around. The crypt door now stood wide open. Alfie stared into the dark well of the staircase, his heart crashing against his ribs, his breathing sharp and shallow. A grey shape slowly emerged from the darkness.

Alfie ran for the main doors, his mind empty of everything except the need to run and hide. He heaved the wooden bar up on its pivot. He remembered that the last time he had tried to open these doors from the inside, he had failed. But there was nothing else he could do. He grasped the black ring and turned it.

To Alfie's enormous relief, the ring responded, turning easily in his hands. He yanked on the door and it swung open smoothly. The open night lay beyond: freedom!

A blazing coldness gripped Alfie's arm, burning him to the bone; the monk had grasped his arm with one hand. Alfie fought to get free, twisting and writhing in the freezing grip, but his shoes slipped away under him and he fell heavily over the stone threshold.

A deadly numbness was flowing up his arm and into his shoulder now. Alfie squirmed around on the stones, struggling to get free, kicking and fighting for his life. The monk was stooping over him, the rope looped in one hand. Alfie stared up into the cavern of the hood.

Almost as if it had a life of its own, the noose of rope slipped over his head. Alfie felt it tightening on his neck. A gush of foul air poured from the blackness under the hood, like a gust of putrid, silent laughter. The evil, triumphant laughter of an executioner who has finally caught his victim.

Alfie screamed.

He woke up with a jolt, his fingers clawing at his throat, his whole body drenched with sweat. His pulse thundered in his ears as he stared wide-eyed into the darkness of the bedroom.

A few moments later, he was blinded by a burst of light.

'Alfie?' It was his gran. She had switched the light on. 'Are you all right?' She came running to his bedside.

He stared at her, his vision swimming. 'Yes,' he managed to gasp. 'It was a dream . . . a bad dream.'

His gran sat on the edge of the bed, her hand to her chest. She had thrown a dressing-gown over her nightclothes, and her hair was all on end from sleep. 'Oh, you did frighten me for a moment,' she said. She looked at him. 'A nightmare?'

Alfie nodded, gradually feeling himself calming down as he looked into her friendly, anxious face. 'Pretty scary,' he admitted.

'Shall I sit with you for a while?' his gran asked. 'Or would you like a nice hot drink?'

'No, I'm fine now,' he said. 'It's OK. You can go back to bed.'

She smiled. 'Sure?'

'Positive.'

She got up. 'If you feel a bit spooked, you can always go downstairs and make yourself something to eat or watch some telly,' she said.

Alfie nodded. 'OK, thanks,' he said.

Granny Dorry switched the light off and closed the door. Alfie listened to the soft sound of her feet padding along the landing. There was the click of her bedroom door closing, and then silence.

Alfie lay in the dark for a few moments, his eyes wide open. He hadn't wanted his gran to fuss and worry, but he knew the nightmare was still lurking nearby – like a monster under the bed – just waiting for him to close his eyes.

He sat up. His throat was sore, and when he touched his neck with his fingertips, it felt tender and uncomfortable. He had woken with his hands up to his neck; he guessed he must have gripped his own throat in his sleep.

That was a nasty idea. Last night he had banged his knee, tonight he had almost throttled himself. Alfie threw the bedcovers off and got up. No way was he ever going to sleep in that room again. He didn't care if it was the craziest thing in the world, there was definitely something weird about the place. He never had dreams like this at home. Next time Mum had to go away overnight, Granny Dorry could just come over to their place to sleep.

Alfie dressed quickly in the dark and padded downstairs. The hall clock showed that it was ten past five. Dawn was a little way off yet. He went into the kitchen, opened the fridge and poured himself a glass of juice. Then he went through to the living-room and switched on the light. Surrounded by his gran's cosy old furniture, the terrors of his nightmare began to fade away, but Alfie still had no intention of returning to his bedroom before the sun came up.

He knew his gran wouldn't mind him having a rummage around in the games cabinet. Maybe he would find a game he could play to while away the time – if there was one without pieces missing.

He knelt on the carpet, emptying the games out

one by one. Nothing really took his fancy. The old photo albums were in the cupboard too, lying on a black cardboard box. He lifted the albums out and put them on the carpet. Curiously, he reached in and took hold of the box. It wasn't very big – about the size of a shoebox, only shallower.

He took the lid off the box. It had more photos in it. He was about to put the lid back on when the top picture caught his eye. The photo was of a couple of kids: a boy and a girl. He guessed that the boy must have been about his age. The little girl was holding his hand, and looked around four or five years old.

The thing that had caught Alfie's attention was the fact that the boy looked a lot like *him*. He had totally different hair, and he wore old-fashioned clothes, but he had a very similar smile and the same shaped face.

Alfie turned the picture over. Someone had written 'Martin and Suzanna' on the back in black Biro. Suzanna was his mum's name. Alfie realized he was looking at a picture of his mum and her older brother.

He quickly put the photo back in the box; there was something unsettling about the picture. The boy looked really cheerful, but Alfie knew that Martin must have died shortly after the picture had been taken. A chill trickled down his spine.

A newspaper cutting poked out from under the photos. Curiously, Alfie drew it out and unfolded it. The headline was *Budding Artist Wins Gallery Prize*, and there was a grainy black and white picture of Martin standing next to a painting of the ruined abbey. Oddly enough, it looked as though Martin had painted his picture from almost the same position as Alfie's painting of the day before.

Intrigued, Alfie read the short article under the picture:

Ten-year-old Martin Bryce has been proclaimed winner of this year's Young Artist Award for his outstanding watercolour of Fosdyke Abbey, pictured above. Despite his obvious talent, when asked, Martin said he did not want to grow up to be an artist, but would rather play football for Manchester United.

Alfie stopped reading – it was too sad knowing that Martin wasn't going to grow up to be anything at all. As he went to put the clipping back in the box, a second clipping made his heart miss a beat. He picked it up.

There was a smaller picture of Martin this time, under the heading *Tragic Death Of Young Artist Award Winner*. Reluctantly, Alfie read the article:

Martin Bryce, the ten-year-old who only last week won the local Young Artist Award, was found dead in his bed by his mother yesterday morning. A police doctor who attended the scene pronounced that Martin's death was due to strangulation by his own bed sheet. The distraught parents told the police that Martin had been experiencing bad dreams for some days before the tragedy, and that they were often awoken by his screams to find him twisting and writhing in his sleep. The police believe that by a tragic accident, Martin became tangled in his sheets and died of strangulation before his parents could come to his aid.

Alfie's hand was shaking as he put the terrible newspaper clipping back in the box and closed the lid on it. For several long minutes, he just sat there numbly, staring at the carpet.

In his mind, he saw his own painting of the abbey, disfigured by the grey smear that might be a rain-smudge . . . or might be something else entirely!

At last, he took a deep breath and began to put everything back into the cabinet. He had no idea what to make of his Uncle Martin's death, and he really, *really* didn't want to think about his own bad dreams in that awful room.

Alfie closed the cabinet door and went out to sit in the garden. The sky was pale grey with the coming dawn. Just a few more hours now and Mum would come to pick him up and take him home. He decided he wasn't going to speak to anyone about his nightmares. If he didn't ever talk about them, then perhaps he could forget they had ever happened.

But one thing was for certain – no way was he taking that painting home with him. It could stay up in that room, and the ghostly monk could stay with it!

'So, Alfie, it wasn't so bad being without the TV for one little weekend, was it now?' his mum asked.

Alfie looked at her as she drove them home later that afternoon. 'No, it wasn't *so* bad,' he said. 'But next time, can Granny Dorry come to our place, please?'

'If you like. Do you want to hear about my course, then?'

Alfie smiled, relieved and delighted to be sitting next to his mum in their little car and heading for home. 'If you like.'

His mum began to talk about her experiences in Birmingham. Alfie only half listened. He had other things on his mind. He had done his best to behave normally in front of his gran that morning, although it hadn't been easy. They had gone for a long walk up on the hills, and that had helped to clear the dark thoughts out of his mind. He had only gone up to Martin's room once more, and that had been to throw his things into his holdall when his mum had arrived.

I am not going to think about the nightmares any more, he said to himself every time the shadows started to grow in his mind. *If I don't think about them, everything will be fine.*

And it seemed to work. When they got home, Alfie dived straight into the living-room and spent the next hour or so with his PlayStation. That was more like it! A few good explosions and an attempt on level five of his new shoot-'em-up game was just what he needed.

He started yawning pretty early. The two restless nights in Martin's old room had left him feeling wiped out. So much so that Alfie didn't even offer any protests when his mum suggested he go to bed half an hour earlier than usual.

It was a cloudy, sticky kind of night, and even with his bedroom window open and the curtains wide, the air was thick and heavy. Alfie lay under his duvet for a few minutes, blissfully happy to be back in his own bed, but too hot to feel comfortable, even with both feet sticking out.

After a little while he gave up, sat up and undid the poppers along the bottom of his duvet cover. He dragged the duvet out and threw it on the floor, then lay back, pulling the empty cover over himself. *That's better*, he thought contentedly, and soon he was drifting off to sleep.

* * *

Alfie was half aware of the sound of the doorbell just as he was dozing off. He thought he heard his gran's voice down in the hall and he wondered woozily why she had come, but he was too sleepy now to give it much thought.

'*Goa-a-al!*' Alfie cheered in delight. Not only had he scored a brilliant scissor-kick goal, but the opposing goalkeeper had been the ghost monk and he'd whacked him right in his rotten invisible face with the speeding football, flattening him out in the goalmouth like a ghost pancake! It *was* a bit odd that they were playing the inter-school championship game in the abbey churchyard, but Alfie couldn't have cared less where they were as he ran triumphantly around the strange pitch, leaping over gravestones and punching the air and yelling at the top of his voice.

'Alfie, shush now.' It was his mother's voice. *What's she doing on the pitch?* Alfie asked himself.

He woke up, aware of a gentle hand on his

forehead. His room was in darkness, but he could just make out his mother's face in the light that filtered through the doorway.

'You were talking in your sleep,' his mum told him.

'I scored the winner,' Alfie mumbled drowsily. 'It was great.'

'I bet it was,' she said softly. 'Go back to sleep now – you clever thing. I never knew you were so talented.'

Talented? Alfie wondered sleepily. *What is she talking about?* Then he realized that she must have meant the football dream and a few seconds later he was asleep again.

He was running through the night, panting as he made his way up a steep wooded hillside. At the crest of the hill he risked a glance over his shoulder. He could see the dim grey abbey walls far below him, like rotten teeth in the pitiless night. But it was the grey shadow, gliding effortlessly upwards through the trees, that held his fearful gaze.

With a groan of horror, Alfie began running again, down the other side of the hill. Through the thinning trees below him, he could see the wide expanse of the disused industrial estate.

He tumbled helter-skelter down the hillside and leaped at the rusty wire fence. He hardly knew where he was getting the strength from – pure fear, probably – but he managed to swarm up the fence and over it in a few frantic moments. He jumped down on to the grey tarmac and sprinted off through the car-wrecks and piles of rubble.

The empty factory buildings towered over him, rows and rows of smashed windows staring down at him as he stumbled and staggered onwards. He had only one thought in his mind – to get home.

If he could only stay ahead of his pursuer till he got to his own house – to his own *room* – then Alfie felt sure he would be safe at last.

He glanced back. The monk was right behind him. The wire fence had been no barrier at all.

Alfie came to the corrugated iron fencing that separated the industrial estate from the town. He knew there was a gap in it somewhere, but where? He ran along the fence, looking, and then he saw it: a v-shaped slot in the fence, only a couple of metres away. It was small, but wide enough for him to squirm through on his stomach.

He didn't look back again; he didn't want to know how close the monk was. He just threw himself down on his front and wriggled under the fence, expecting to feel the ice-cold grip of the ghost's hand on his ankle at any moment.

Safely through, Alfie leaped to his feet and ran for home. It wasn't far now. He pounded along his own street, gasping for breath, using up his very last reserves of strength.

Thankfully, his front door was open. Alfie stumbled over the threshold and ran for the stairs. For some reason it never occurred to him to call to his mum for help. It was as if he was engaged in a deadly game of tag that nobody else could play, and if he could only get to his room, it would all be over.

Finally, he staggered through the doorway of his bedroom. To Alfie's surprise, he found it lit by two rows of tall, thick bone-white candles that formed a kind of aisle across the room. Alfie slowed to a walk. The corridor of candles led to the far side of his bed, where more candles flickered on his bedside table. Their light fell on a painting that was propped there.

Alfie frowned in confusion; he never had candles in his room. He walked slowly down the aisle of candles and stared at the painting on his bedside table. It was the picture he had painted of the old abbey. The picture with the grey smear . . .

Alfie woke up, drenched with sweat, and a sudden new panic filled his heart. He turned over, and in the dim morning light he saw his painting, propped up on his bedside table.

His heart pounded. That was why his gran had

called round, he realized in horror, and that was why his mother had been in his room earlier. Granny Dorry had brought his painting over, and his mum had brought it up to his room. He remembered her words: 'you clever thing, I never knew you were so talented'. She hadn't been talking about his dream-goal, she had been talking about the painting.

And even as Alfie stared at the picture in alarm, it seemed to come alive. He watched, frozen in terror, as the grey smear of the monk began to move towards him.

Slowly, unstoppably, the monk approached, growing larger and larger.

Alfie tried to scream, but his throat was constricted and nothing came out. He could do nothing but stare as the ghastly figure actually stepped *out* of the painting and stood towering over him in the real world, at his bedside.

The grey rope glinted in the monk's hands as he leaned down close to Alfie. And Alfie stared transfixed into the utter blackness where the monk's face should have been. He felt the rope slide around his neck and begin to tighten . . .

Alfie knew that it was too late, just as he now knew exactly what had happened to his Uncle Martin, strangled by the ghost monk of Fosdyke Abbey – in his dreams.

THE RACE

Annabel Cole gave a sigh of relief as the bell sounded for the end of the final lesson of the school day. She slapped her maths textbook closed, picked up her schoolbag and shovelled her books and pencil-case into it.

Maths! What was the point? No point at all, so far as she could see. She stood up, gazing out of the window. From here she could see out over the school playing-fields and the tennis courts and football pitches. Some boys were out there now – kicking a ball around.

If there were any justice in the world, Annabel thought, she'd be in the boy's school team. She was as good at football as any boy, but there were idiotic rules that meant mixed teams weren't allowed. Not that Annabel was particularly bothered about being excluded from the boys' team. She was *captain* of the girls' team, and the real love of her life was her running.

She retied the red ribbon that held her long dark hair in a ponytail, slung her bag over her shoulder and joined the throng of people struggling to get out of the form room.

Out in the corridor she saw Kelly Hazeldene and Zoë Winters. Kelly was a good friend – Zoë less so. Annabel's grandad said Zoë sounded like she'd spent the night in the knife drawer – she was so sharp she'd have to watch she didn't cut herself. Annabel liked the odd things her grandad said.

Kelly came bouncing up, her blonde hair bobbing. 'Hi, Annabel!' she sang out. 'A bunch of us are going to the pizza parlour. Do you want to come?'

Annabel hesitated. It sounded like fun, but she had already made a promise to her coach, Mr McNabb . . .

'Come on,' Kelly said, smiling encouragingly at Annabel. 'It'll be great.'

Zoë shook her head. 'She won't be able to come. She's probably got to go *running* again, because running is so much more fun than hanging out with real *people!*'

Annabel gave her a weary smile – that was typical Zoë! Luckily, Zoë spotted a friend in the crowd and rushed off to talk to her.

Kelly frowned at Annabel. '*Are* you going running?' she asked.

Annabel gave a regretful shrug. 'I promised Mr McNabb I'd go to training. He'll be expecting me.'

Kelly sighed. 'Listen, Annabel, if you don't hang

out with your friends *occasionally*, we're just going to give up on you!'

Annabel smiled apologetically. 'I'm sorry,' she replied. 'I can't let Mr McNabb down today. There's a big race coming up at the weekend. How about next week?'

Kelly laughed. 'OK, it's a deal!' she agreed, and with a wave, she was gone.

Annabel took a deep breath. The crowds had thinned out now, and she was standing alone in the corridor. *Even Kelly doesn't really get it*, she thought sadly. The only one who really understood was her coach, Mr McNabb. He knew what it was like: the beautiful, effortless rhythm Annabel would get into on a long run, the way her feet would just seem to bounce her along the track, the controlled breathing – in through the nose, out through the mouth – her eyes on the road ahead, her brain totally focused on the winning-post. And even in a hard run, when she wanted to give up, there was that moment when she broke through the pain barrier, when she got her second wind and it gave her such a rush that she felt like she could go on running for ever.

Annabel glanced at her watch. Oops! If she wasn't quick she'd be late for her practice session, and Mr McNabb was a stickler for punctuality. She turned on her heel and ran along the corridor, her ribbon streaming out behind her.

'You're five minutes late!' Mr McNabb said, as Annabel came jogging over in her running kit.

'Sorry,' she said. 'I got held up.'

Mr McNabb frowned at her. She knew he didn't mean to frown; he just had that kind of face – a face that reminded Annabel of rugged cliffs. It was weather-beaten, and full of lines and creases and interesting folds. He also had a wild thatch of dark-brown hair that stuck out at all angles, and piercing blue eyes. Annabel guessed that he was probably about forty. He was in quite good shape for an old guy; he could still do a sprint start that would leave most people standing. But he'd given up competing ages ago. Annabel wasn't sure why.

'Listen to me, Annabel,' he said, towering over her in his grey track suit. 'You could have a great future as an athlete – and that's not something I say to many people, believe me – but it's up to you. If you train hard and maintain focus and discipline, well, I can see you in the Olympics a few years from now. You're potentially that good.' He raised a large, warning finger. '*Potentially!* You know what I mean by "potentially", don't you?'

'Yes,' Annabel said quite meekly. She'd had this lecture before. 'It means that it's all up to me. If I do the work, I'll make it. If I don't, I won't.' She looked at him. 'I was only five minutes late.'

'Late is late,' he replied. 'And right now you can't allow yourself to be distracted by anything. Not with the qualifiers for the National Junior Squad only three days away. You need to be coming into peak form right now. Peak too early and you lose the race, peak too late and you lose the race. Peak at exactly the right moment and—'

'I win, win, win!' Annabel interrupted, jumping up in the air and giving a victory punch.

Mr McNabb smiled. 'That's the girl!' he said. He thumped his chest. 'It's all down to heart. It's all down to self-belief. But you're going to have some stiff competition out there on the day.'

Annabel came back down to earth. She knew exactly who he meant. 'Ophelia Levesque!' she said.

'Exactly.' He put his huge hand on Annabel's shoulder. 'What's your biggest psychological disadvantage when it comes to facing Ophelia?'

'The fact that I've never beaten her,' Annabel said gloomily. Ophelia was County Champion. She had speed and stamina and an ability to focus that it seemed nobody else in their division could match. They had run the 400 metres against each other on three separate occasions, and each time Annabel had been leading, only to see Ophelia go zipping past her at the last moment.

'It's important that you don't focus too much on Ophelia,' Mr McNabb said. 'What have I always told you about running?'

'That the only person I'm competing against is myself,' Annabel recited. 'But I can't just wish Ophelia away. I have to beat her!'

'And you will,' Mr McNabb said. 'But you need some help.'

'Tell me about it!' Annabel sighed.

'Self-help,' Mr McNabb continued, reaching out a forefinger and lightly tapping her on the forehead. 'Help from in here.'

Annabel looked at him, puzzled.

He smiled. 'I'll let you into a little secret,' he said. 'It'll make all the difference – you'll see.'

Annabel tightened the bow on her red ribbon. She put her toe to the line, stretching out her other leg for a power push-off, leaning in low, her eyes focused on the long curve of the racetrack ahead.

'Focus. Concentrate. Work,' called Mr McNabb. He clapped his hands together.

Annabel sprang forwards, arms pumping at her sides, getting quickly into the rhythm of the run, bending herself into the curve, making sure she kept between the lines of her lane. *Stray out of your lane and it's instant disqualification*, Annabel reminded herself.

She lifted her chin and tried to concentrate on the technique that Mr McNabb had explained to her. She heard his voice in her head: 'Visualize another runner in your mind. Try to see her on the track ahead of you. Chase her. Run her down. She's always ahead of you – just out of reach. When you speed up, she speeds up. She wants you to work, to stretch yourself, to run like you've never run before.'

Annabel stared at the track ahead of her, trying to conjure up the image of another runner. But no matter how hard she tried, the track remained empty. There was no one else there.

How did Mr McNabb expect her to do this? She couldn't trick herself into seeing someone who wasn't there. It sounded very silly. And then, as she rounded the bend and started heading back to where Mr McNabb was waiting with a stopwatch in his hand, she suddenly had an image in her mind.

The only problem was that the girl Annabel could imagine flying away up ahead of her was Ophelia Levesque. Ophelia even glanced over her shoulder and gave that annoying smile of hers as she swept over the finish line, throwing her arms in the air as she slowed to a triumphant halt.

Annabel crossed the finish line herself and slowed to a stop, bending over and sucking in air, her hands on her knees.

'Not good enough,' came Mr McNabb's voice. 'You can do a lot better than that.'

'I don't . . . think . . . that technique of yours is going . . . to work . . .' Annabel panted, straightening up.

'Take a break, then we'll try it again,' Mr McNabb replied.

'I can't do it,' Annabel protested.

'Yes, you can,' Mr McNabb insisted. 'The technique works. I used to use it myself, years ago, when I was your age. I learned it from a brilliant runner. She was a real winner.'

Annabel looked at him with new interest. Mr McNabb had never talked about his days as a young athlete, even when she had pestered him for stories. She knew he'd been good – but she had no idea how good, or why he had stopped running.

'Who was she?' she asked.

'A friend of mine from way back,' Mr McNabb said dismissively. 'No one you'd have heard of. She died when she was very young.'

'Oh.' Annabel looked at him curiously. 'What distance did she like to run?'

Mr McNabb gave her one of his heavy frowns. 'Are you rested enough to give it another try yet?'

'Well, yes, but—'

'Off you go, then,' he interrupted. 'We're not here to chat, we're here to work.'

So much for finding out about Mr McNabb's glory days! Annabel stood on the start line again, shaking her arms to relax the muscles, turning her head on her neck to ease out any stiffness. Then she took up the start position again, staring along the white lines.

Clap!

Off she went, running well this time as she leaned into the bend, feet pounding, arms working. She tried to imagine her invisible opponent just up ahead.

And she was *almost* successful! A speeding figure began to take shape – getting more solid as Annabel focused on the kicking heels and the flying hair. It still looked a lot like Ophelia, but that wasn't really a surprise. She focused on the indistinct runner ahead of her – trying to catch her. She was working hard now, concentrating.

'Whoa!' Annabel heard Mr McNabb's voice as

she sprinted past him. She'd crossed the finish line without even realizing it. She pulled up and trotted over to where he was standing.

'Much better!' he said. 'That was your fastest time this year!'

'I could almost see her that time,' Annabel panted with a grin. 'Give me five minutes, then I want to try that again.'

Maybe Mr McNabb is on to something after all, she thought. And as the session progressed, so Annabel's phantom opponent seemed to get more and more solid.

Each time she ran, Annabel felt that she was getting just a fraction closer to the speeding girl. Her speeds around the track gradually got better and better and she was determined that one day she would catch her imaginary rival.

Mr McNabb was a stickler for doing things right – which was why Annabel was jogging home at the end of her training session. It was part of her warm-down routine, a good way of getting all the excess lactose out of her muscles. She knew that stopping exercise abruptly was as dangerous as starting without warming up. You could do damage that it might take weeks to put right.

Mr McNabb had suggested that she should head on down to the County Stadium before school the next morning, to get herself used to the look and the feel of the place where she would be running on Saturday. Annabel thought it sounded like a good idea.

'What do you think, Speedy-Edie?' she called out to the imaginary girl who was also jogging home just ahead of her. The girl looked around and grinned.

'You're going to be really helpful, you know?' Annabel told the girl cheerfully. 'Between us, we're going to beat Ophelia. You bet we are!'

And then the oddest thing happened. Annabel rounded a corner and saw Ophelia Levesque up ahead of her, right in the middle of the pavement, doing stretching exercises. Speedy-Edie evaporated and Annabel came to a gentle halt. 'Hello there,' she said.

Ophelia looked up at her and smiled. 'Hi!' she replied, shaking her legs and bouncing on the spot. 'Going my way?'

'Sure,' Annabel confirmed. Although she went to a different school, Annabel knew that Ophelia lived only a couple of streets away from her. Despite the fact that they were rivals on the track, Annabel rather liked the other girl; Ophelia was someone who really understood the appeal of running.

They jogged on together quite contentedly. Annabel wondered whether to tell Ophelia about Mr McNabb's training technique, but then decided not to. She was pretty certain that Ophelia didn't have an invisible running opponent, and Annabel wasn't about to let her in on such a useful secret.

'So,' Ophelia said as they jogged along side by

side. 'It's the Big One this weekend. Is Mr McNabb giving you a hard time about it?'

'No more than usual,' Annabel replied. 'How about your coach?'

Ophelia sighed. 'Miss West keeps going on about how important this race is – how I have to pace myself so that I'm at my peak on the day.' She gave her voice a nasal twang. 'Ophelia, you gotta literally go for it on the day, know what I mean? You gotta literally win the race in your head before you even get on the track.' She laughed, and Annabel laughed too – Ophelia did a good impersonation of her coach.

'Mr McNabb's like that all the time,' Annabel said. She deepened her voice, speaking from her stomach. 'Work! Concentrate! Focus!'

Both girls laughed again.

'Hey, there's a long, straight stretch of road up ahead,' Ophelia said. 'Want to run it – just for a laugh?'

Annabel hesitated, tempted to take up the

challenge, but decided against it – the last thing she needed right now was to lose to Ophelia only days before the Big Race! She shook her head. 'Let's save it for Saturday,' she said.

'Fair enough,' Ophelia agreed.

They continued to jog along together in friendly silence, shoulder to shoulder, stride for stride.

Annabel lay in bed that night, her hands behind her head, staring at the huge poster on the wall opposite her.

It was a photo of her all-time running hero, Vanessa Page. Vanessa had won the Gold in the 400 metres at the last Olympic Games. The poster was a shot of her taking the line, and you could see from the expression on her face that she knew she had won: joy, delight and triumph shone in her eyes.

Annabel knew that she actually looked a bit like Vanessa. She had the same long black hair and the same dark eyes. One day, maybe, there would be a girl lying in bed gazing up at a poster of *her* winning Gold! Now that was something to work for.

Under the picture in big red letters was the slogan for which Vanessa had become famous: 'GIVE IT ALL YOUR HEART!'

Annabel smiled as she read the words, and for a few moments all her worries about Ophelia seemed to melt away. 'I can beat her,' she told the frozen winning face on the poster. 'And I *will* beat her! I will give it all my heart!'

Annabel was used to getting up early in the morning to do an hour's training before school. She enjoyed the early-morning runs, when there were hardly any people about. The grass was still wet with dew and on cloudless days, like this one, the low sun was bright and sharp in her eyes.

Today, as she jogged down to the stadium, Annabel imagined Speedy-Edie, pale and insubstantial in the bright morning light, but running smoothly and steadily a couple of metres ahead of her.

She was so focused on the wispy figure that it was quite a shock when a far more substantial shape suddenly loomed into view, and Annabel was even more surprised to see that it was her grandad.

She came to a halt in front of him, bouncing up and down to keep her muscles warm. 'Hi there!' she said with a smile. 'What are you doing out this early?'

'I often enjoy a nice quiet walk this time of day,' said her grandad. He raised a questioning eyebrow. 'You don't usually come this way on your runs.'

'I'm going to the stadium,' Annabel explained, her ponytail bouncing on her shoulders as she jogged on the spot. 'We've got a big meet there on Saturday. Did Mum tell you?'

'Yes, she did,' her grandad said. 'And I'll be there to cheer you on. So you're off to the stadium now, eh? Well, did you know that there used to be illegal boxing matches in the very field where they built that stadium?'

Annabel shook her head.

'Brutal stuff, it was, bare-knuckle fighting, and as many rounds as it took for one chap to knock the other out. My dad told me about one match he saw when he was a boy. It was between a local lad, Billy Rhys, and a real monster of a man called The Scrapper. Six foot one inch, he was, with fists like hammers. A lot of money changed hands on that match – I remember my dad telling me – thousands of pounds. But it all had to be done in secret, because the police would have broken it up if they'd known.'

Annabel usually loved listening to her grandad's tales, but today she was impatient to get on with her run. 'Who won?' she asked, hoping to bring the story to a quick conclusion.

'Billy Rhys did,' her grandad told her. 'After fifteen rounds and with one eye bunged up with blood and gore.'

'Ewww!'

'I told you it was a brutal sport. But Billy caught The Scrapper a good one – a clean right-hander to the heart – and The Scrapper went down like a felled tree.' Her grandad's eyes glinted as he looked at her, nodding gloomily. 'And he didn't ever get up again, my girl. Think about that! Down he went, and that was that.'

Annabel stared at him. 'He was killed, you mean?' she gasped.

Her grandad nodded again. 'That was the last of the bare-knuckle fights. It couldn't be hushed up – not a death. And then the council bought the land and built the stadium. But it's a bad place. It's got bad memories – that's why that young girl died, if you ask me.'

Annabel stopped jogging. 'Grandad, what are you talking about?' she asked, feeling quite creeped out by his stories. 'What girl?'

'It was some years back – when your Uncle David was about the age you are now. I was at the stadium for an inter-school meet. Some lad was shooting his mouth off – saying that girls could never run as fast as boys – and there was this one girl who took him up on the challenge. She bet him she'd beat him in a fair race. So they went for it – the pair of them.' His voice dropped. 'Of course, no one had any idea of what was going to happen. They ran the race, the girl won by a whisker, but then she just collapsed on the track, just after she'd crossed the finish line. People ran to help, but it was too late – the poor girl was stone-dead!'

Annabel's eyes were wide with amazement. 'Is that a true story, Grandad?' she whispered.

'True as I'm standing here,' he replied. 'It was in the local papers and everything. They did a post-mortem to find out what killed her, and the doctors said her heart had just burst! They reckoned she had some sort of congenital weakness.' He shook his head. 'It was a shock, I can tell you. They even considered closing the stadium at one point. I don't remember the poor girl's name, but I can still see her in my mind's eye – racing around that track, full of life, her golden hair flying out behind her.'

'That's a sad story,' Annabel said. 'I've never heard about it before.'

'People prefer to forget,' her grandad told her. 'Especially tragic things like that.' He smiled at her. 'But it was a long, long time ago, girl. Don't let it upset you. Go on, I can see you're raring to get over there. Don't let my silly old stories put you off.'

'I won't,' Annabel said. 'See you Saturday.'

'That you will,' he called as she ran off.

Maybe it was because of her grandad's creepy stories, but Annabel felt that the small County Stadium had an eerie quality in the early-morning light. Wisps of mist floated across the oval field, somehow making the curving grey of the track look slightly unreal. Above her, the towering floodlights hung over the stadium like clawing skeletal hands.

Annabel jogged in through a gap in the raised seating, feeling a chill breeze swirl around her ankles. It was easy to imagine two sturdy, bare-fisted fighters slugging it out in the middle of the atheletics field. She shuddered; she could almost hear the horrible dull sound of bloody fists striking flesh and bone, amid the roar of the crowd.

She did one gentle lap of the track, taking it easy, clearing her mind of those grim thoughts. *I should be thinking about the crowds that'll be here on Saturday*, she told herself. 'Raaaahhh! Anna-*bel*! Anna-*bel*! Champi-*on*! Champi-*on*!' she cheered. Then she waved her arms in the air, grinning around at the invisible crowd as she jogged up to the start line. That was more like it.

She got into position to start running for real: toe to the line, back bent into the long curve of the track, eyes focused on the thin stretch of grey ahead of her.

'The crowd quietens down,' she murmured.

'They can feel the tension as the great race begins. Any moment now!'

She heard an imaginary starter's gun in her head, pressed the timer button on her wristwatch and shot forward, striving to get into a good rhythm as quickly as possible.

Annabel was surprised to see her imaginary running companion up ahead of her in the next lane. She hadn't really been thinking about Speedy-Edie; her imaginary rival had just popped up out of nowhere. The mist curled around her, but this time Annabel could see details about the girl that she had never noticed before, and she didn't look one little bit like Ophelia now. She looked about the same age and height as Annabel, and she had blonde hair. She was in white running gear and she had a number pinned to her back: 619.

Why 619? Annabel wondered as she stared at the girl through the mist. What the significance of that number was she had absolutely no idea. She supposed her imagination must have dragged the number up from some dark corner of her mind, but it meant nothing to her. How odd.

Then Annabel noticed something even more odd. The girl was carrying a baton, as if she were part of a relay race. Now that really was weird. Annabel had never taken part in a relay. It wasn't her thing. So why did her imaginary race rival have a baton?

She remembered one of her grandad's sayings: the mind can play funny tricks on you. Well, right now, her mind was certainly playing tricks on her, and Annabel figured it was time she played some tricks back. She lengthened her stride, getting into sprint-finish mode. It was far too early in the race to be doing that, but she wanted to catch up with her imaginary opponent and blast her right off the track!

She gained ground on the girl – lessening the gap from five metres to two. But then the girl gave a kick of her own and pulled smoothly away from Annabel again.

'Oh, no, you don't!' muttered Annabel. She moved up a gear herself, running flat out now and reducing the gap again. Two metres, one – she had almost caught up with her opponent . . . And then she was across the finish line!

She jabbed at her watch to stop the timer as she came to a gradual halt. The imaginary girl had melted away.

Annabel folded up, hands on knees, gasping for breath. 'I'll get you next time!' she panted. Then she laughed breathlessly. 'That was some race!' She glanced at her time. It was unbelievable!

She straightened and stood there in the chilly mist, peering at her watch in disbelief. 'No way!' she gasped. 'No . . . way!' Either the watch was wrong, or she had just run the fastest race of her entire life! She grinned to herself; she knew there was nothing wrong with her watch.

'I was wondering,' Annabel asked Mr McNabb. 'What if I beat her?'

It was lunch break at school. Annabel had sought her coach out in his small office in the gym block. She just couldn't wait to tell him how well his technique had worked that morning, and about the astonishing times she'd clocked up against Speedy-Edie.

Mr McNabb smiled at her from behind his desk. 'You'll never catch her,' he said. 'But you're thinking along the right lines.'

Annabel persisted. 'But what if I *do*?' she asked. 'My grandad told me once that if racing greyhounds ever actually catch the hare, they never run well again. I'm just worried that if I catch Edie, the same will happen to me.'

'Edie?'

'I call her that,' Annabel said with a shrug. 'Speedy-Edie. It's just a name.'

'The reason you'll never catch her is because she's *you*,' Mr McNabb explained. 'She's a mental representation of your own desire to win. She's the *perfect* you, if you like. She's what you want to be –

and no one can ever catch up with what they *want* to be. It's impossible.'

Annabel stared at him, trying to work that out. 'So, you're saying she's the dream me – the me that *always* wins.'

'Exactly,' Mr McNabb said. 'The fantasy version of Annabel Cole.'

'I get it,' Annabel said, smiling slowly. 'Yes – I like that.'

'Now, go. I've got work to do. I'll see you on the track this afternoon.' A grin split his craggy face. 'Both of you!'

Annabel was halfway back to the main school building before it occurred to her to wonder why Speedy-Edie had blonde hair. If she was *Perfect Annabel* like Mr McNabb had said, then why didn't she have Annabel's long, black hair?

And then Annabel realized why – of course, she had always wanted blonde hair, so the perfect Annabel in her mind had to be blonde. Problem solved.

But as she ran around the school track later that afternoon, it seemed to Annabel that maybe her problems weren't as completely solved as she'd thought. She tried and tried to visualize Edie, but her imaginary opponent simply wouldn't take shape. Earlier that morning, it had been easy to see her running along up ahead, always a fraction out of reach, but now the track remained resolutely empty. The best Annabel could manage was a weak image of Ophelia Levesque, and it didn't spur her on to a particularly fast time.

Mr McNabb looked at his watch. 'Good,' he said. 'But not great.'

Annabel could see he wasn't particularly impressed by her times. Neither was she – she'd done so much better earlier. 'Come on, Edie,' she muttered to herself as she prepared for another lap. 'Don't let me down now.'

But Edie didn't show.

Annabel was dispirited as she jogged home that afternoon. Was it *her*? Had she peaked too soon, just like Mr McNabb was always warning? Had she run her best-ever race that morning at the stadium?

And where was Speedy-Edie? Would she ever come back?

Only Saturday at the stadium would tell.

Annabel tightened her red ribbon as she walked to the start line for the first of her two qualifying heats.

This was it. The County Stadium was packed and there was a real buzz in the air. Now, more than ever, Annabel had to keep focused on her race. Other competitors filled the grassy oval around which the track looped. Plenty of field events were underway: high jump, javelin, discus and long jump.

It was hard to imagine that this was the same place that had seemed so creepy to Annabel in the early-morning mist just a couple of days ago. Her mum, dad and grandad were there in the crowd – standing at the rail – waving and smiling as the starter called the competitors for the first heat of the 400 metres.

The good news was that Annabel was not running against Ophelia at this stage. They weren't due to compete with one another till the final – assuming they both made it that far.

Annabel ignored the competitors lined up against her, focusing entirely on the track itself. She had to come in fourth or better, otherwise she'd be out of the competition for a place on the national team. She was determined not to let that happen.

When the starting gun fired, Annabel went off like a rocket. She saw the poster of Vanessa Page in front of her with its slogan: 'GIVE IT ALL YOUR HEART!' Yes, Annabel thought. *I'm definitely going to do that today. No problem!*

And then, suddenly, Speedy-Edie was there ahead of her – her blonde hair bobbing as she raced along, the wind making the paper number 619 on her back flutter.

What *did* that mean? Annabel wondered, and then quickly decided that she didn't care – Edie was back, that was all that mattered. Annabel lengthened her stride, hardly even aware that she had now pulled way ahead of the rest of the runners. All her attention was concentrated on Edie's back.

She won the race easily and pulled up with cheers and applause ringing in her ears. Speedy-Edie was jogging to a halt up ahead, turning to look back at Annabel and smiling a little, as if she was pleased that Annabel hadn't caught up.

Mr McNabb was delighted with her effort, but somehow Annabel couldn't help feeling she hadn't done as well as she might. She looked at her coach. 'I can do better!' she told him. 'I'm going to beat her!'

Mr McNabb frowned, obviously puzzled that Annabel wasn't better pleased with her performance. 'Beat her?' he echoed. 'Who?'

'Edie!' Annabel replied. 'I'm going to beat her!'

Mr McNabb shook his head. 'You'll never outrun her,' he said. 'You can't.'

Annabel gave him a steely look. That settled it! If there was one thing that had always given her the determination to better herself, it was when someone told her it couldn't be done. 'I'll beat her in the next heat,' Annabel said with absolute conviction. 'And then I'm going to wipe the floor with Ophelia.'

Mr McNabb gave her an uneasy look. She ignored him. He hadn't seen that look in Edie's eyes. The look that said – beat me ... if you can!

Annabel lined up for the second of the qualifying rounds. She glanced at her opponents. There were some very good runners alongside her this time. It wasn't going to be a walk-over like the last heat. And the weather had taken a turn for the worse, too. Clouds had come creeping in from the north, covering up the sun and sending goose bumps running up and down Annabel's arms and legs. The stadium now seemed quite grey and dreary.

'I hope the rain keeps off,' Annabel said to the girl next to her, peering up into the gunmetal grey sky.

The girl stared at her. 'What rain?' she said. 'The forecast is sunshine all day.'

Annabel stared at her. 'But—'

But there was no more time to talk. The starter called for them to get ready, and Annabel had no time to waste wondering why no one else seemed to have noticed the deteriorating weather. She had to get her brain into race mode.

Bang!

Annabel shot forward, getting quickly into her stride, finding a smooth, easy rhythm. But this time she was aware that some of the other girls were keeping pace with her – and two were slightly in front. She smiled grimly – one of the two was Edie.

As Annabel locked her eyes on Edie's back, she

was uncomfortably aware of a thin, pale mist that came sweeping down over the racetrack. The weather was really getting bad now. If the mist got any thicker, Annabel thought the whole meet might be called off.

Edie ran on, heedless of the gathering mist. Annabel strove to catch up with her. She was coming closer now, closer to Edie than she had ever been before. So close she felt she could almost reach out and touch her.

Then Edie kicked out and the gap widened.

No! Annabel thought, and somehow found an extra reserve of speed to close the gap once more. Only half a metre separated them now . . .

A sudden shiver ran through Annabel, taking her by surprise and making her stumble. The sudden coldness was enough to cause her to lose her balance and fall awkwardly on to the track.

She gasped for breath as Mr McNabb hurried over to her. 'Are you all right?' he asked, helping her to her feet.

'Yes,' she gasped, and then the realization of what had happened struck her. 'Oh, no!' she exclaimed. 'I *lost*! I'm out of the final.'

'No, you didn't,' said Mr McNabb. 'You won!'

Annabel blinked at him. 'What?'

He chuckled at her. 'Didn't you even realize?' he asked. 'You stumbled just as you crossed the winning line. You came first. You beat the next girl by a clear half-second.'

Annabel's spirits rose immediately and a wide grin spread over her face. 'I did?' she gasped.

'You did!' Mr McNabb said. He pointed to the stands. 'I think there are some people there who'd like to congratulate you!'

She followed the line of his pointing finger. Her mum, dad and grandad were there, waving and applauding. With a smile, she jogged over to talk to them.

'Are you all right?' her mum asked. 'That was quite a tumble!'

'I'm fine,' Annabel said happily.

'You showed them,' said her dad. 'You went around that last bend like you were jet-propelled. You just beat your personal best!'

Annabel grinned at them. 'And I can do even better than that!' she said. 'I've got a secret weapon!'

'What's that, then?' her grandad asked.

'Edie,' said Annabel. 'I'll tell you all about her later.' She looked up into the grey sky. 'I just hope the weather clears up a bit before the final.'

'Clears up a bit?' said her father. 'How much clearer do you want it to be?'

'Warmer would be nice,' Annabel said.

Her mum frowned at her. 'But it's perfectly warm, Annabel,' she said. She reached out a hand and rested it on Annabel's arm. 'Heavens, you *are* cold!' she exclaimed. 'Go and put something on right away.'

Annabel nodded. 'I'll be back in a bit,' she said, jogging off to where she'd left her track suit.

It was really odd how no one else seemed to mind the cold. It was almost as if she was the only one who could feel the chilly breeze. But the weather did seem to be improving a little, she noticed. The mist had evaporated and the clouds looked lighter and fluffier now.

She got into her track suit and did some warming-down exercises. It was half an hour till the final of the 400 metres. That gave her plenty of time to hang out with her family and watch the other sports before she had to warm up for the big race.

Annabel stood on the start line with the other finalists. She was in peak form. She felt ready to take on the world. The only dampener was that the icy mist had come back. There had been half an hour of clear weather, but as soon as the call had come over the loudspeaker for the finalists in the 400 metres to assemble, thin sheets of mist had come crawling in across the stadium.

Annabel felt as if the mist was coming and going just to annoy her, but she had more important things to think about now and she pushed the thought from her mind.

Ophelia was there, two lanes over. Their eyes met for a moment and Annabel smiled. She didn't feel any apprehension about Ophelia any more. Ophelia was no longer the challenge. Speedy-Edie was the challenge. She was the one Annabel had to beat.

Bang!

Annabel didn't get a great start, but even while she was still accelerating and trying to find her rhythm she saw Edie up ahead, running smoothly.

I'll get you this time! Annabel thought. An absolute determination filled her. She dug in, lengthening her stride, breathing in time with her running. She pulled ahead of a couple of her opponents, her eyes still fixed on Edie and the flapping number on her back: 619.

She came around the curve, running well, feeling good, finding her best form now. Only two people remained ahead of her – Edie and a slim, swift shape two lanes away: Ophelia.

Annabel sped around the final bend and found herself alongside Ophelia, but Edie was still two metres ahead and running like the wind.

The finish line was in sight. The excited crowd was roaring in her ears like a stormy sea, but the white lines of her lane were the whole extent of Annabel's world. Nothing else mattered. Nothing else existed.

Ophelia fell behind.

Annabel was catching Edie, drawing closer and closer. She was *so* close now . . . And then coldness flooded through her again – filling her chest. This time it was much, much worse than before. It felt like her body was turning to ice.

No! Not this time! No way! Annabel thought. Edie was only half a metre away now and the finish line was rushing closer. With a final supreme effort, Annabel burst through the pain barrier and slipped past Edie just as she crossed the line.

It was a perfect, triumphant moment. Annabel felt as if she could have gone on running for ever. She felt light as a feather as she lifted her arms and threw back her head in pure delight.

She jogged to a halt. That was odd. The mist had cleared. The clouds were gone. The bright afternoon sun shone down into the stadium, filling it with golden light. But it was absolutely silent! Annabel frowned, confused now. Why couldn't she hear the crowd?

Speedy-Edie jogged past her and dropped the baton at her feet. Annabel stared after her as her phantom rival jogged on around the track. Edie turned and gazed back at her, giving her the strangest look, a kind of haunted look – sad and sympathetic, but also relieved. And then, even as Annabel stared after her in bewilderment, Edie faded away like the mist and was gone.

Annabel stared down at the baton that Edie had dropped at her feet, thinking how weird that was.

And then a scream broke the dream-like quality of the moment.

Annabel turned and stared back down the track. Ophelia Levesque and a couple of the other runners were standing over a crumpled form that lay disturbingly still on the racetrack. One of the finalists had fallen right at the finish line. All thoughts of her amazing victory were banished from Annabel's mind and she began to jog back to see whether she could offer any assistance.

As she got closer she was aware of other people running on to the track, and she could hear her grandfather's voice calling out her name. She looked up and saw her mum, dad and grandfather rushing towards the fallen runner.

'It's OK,' she called. 'I'm fine.' But they didn't seem to hear.

Her father dropped on to his knees beside the stricken competitor, gathering her up into his arms.

What is going on? Annabel wondered. She slowed to a walk, frowning as her gaze fell on Ophelia.

The other girl's face was grey with horror, her hands up to her mouth, her eyes staring.

Who is it on the track? Annabel wondered, stepping into a gap and peering between the gathered people.

In disbelief, Annabel found herself gazing at her own pale face, staring up at her, open-eyed, from her father's lap. Annabel looked down into her own glassy eyes in growing panic. This couldn't be happening. It wasn't possible!

Another man pushed through the huddle of distressed competitors. Annabel recognized him as the on-site doctor. He knelt and pressed two fingers to her neck – to the neck of the *other* Annabel – the Annabel who wasn't the real Annabel.

'That's not me!' she cried, staring around at the anxious faces. She saw her mum, standing next to her dad, her face white with shock.

'There's no pulse,' the doctor said quietly, his voice tense. Annabel stared down at him. 'Lie her flat,' he was telling her father. 'I'll try CPR.'

'CPR?' repeated her mother numbly. 'Isn't that what they do when someone's not *breathing*?'

'NO!' Annabel shouted. 'I'm here! I'm fine! That's not me!' But no one could hear her. She reached out to her mother, but her arms passed right through her. No one could see her. No one could hear her. It was as if they were all ghosts. Or . . . as if *she* was.

Annabel watched as the doctor performed CPR on the lifeless body on the racetrack – *her* lifeless body. Long slow seconds ticked by. Annabel thought she ought to cry or scream, or *something*, but she just stood there blankly, staring down at her own unresponsive body.

After what seemed like a bleak eternity of time, the doctor sat up, a defeated expression on his face. 'I'm sorry,' he said. 'I'm so sorry.'

Annabel stared around at the stricken faces. She saw one man step away from the small huddle. It was Mr McNabb, and there was a look in his eyes that was absolutely terrifying. His lips moved as he backed away, and Annabel followed him, trying to hear what he was saying.

'Not again! Please — not again!' he muttered in despair.

And suddenly Annabel realized that Mr McNabb had been there, all those years ago, when the girl had died. The girl whose heart had burst. *He* had been the boy she had raced against. And *she* had been the friend from whom he had learned the visualization technique.

That was who Annabel had been chasing around the track. Edie wasn't a figment of her own imagination, she was a ghost — a ghost doomed for ever to run and rerun her final race in this haunted stadium, where long ago Billy Rhys had killed The Scrapper with a bare-knuckle blow to his heart.

Annabel turned and stared at the baton that still lay abandoned on the track. Now she understood the meaning of that final look the girl had given her. The phantom runner had been doomed to continue the race . . . until someone beat her. Until someone took her place. And now Annabel was facing the same fate.

She stooped and picked up the baton . . .

CARNIVAL
DANCE

'I am invincible! Bow down to the master!' Adam
Dalston yelled, following his match-winning table-
tennis shot by leaping on to the table, punching
the air and emitting a triumphant cheer that could
be heard from one end of Island Youth Club to the
other.

Martina Burrows gave his defeated opponent,
Sam Ryan, a sympathetic look before laughing at
Adam's antics. Sam was looking at Adam as if he

was suppressing a strong desire to find out whether his friend's mouth was big enough to hold an entire table-tennis bat. The way Adam was yelling, it certainly seemed like a possibility.

But that was Adam all over. Rob said that Adam 'evidenced a lamentable surplus of personality' – basically, he was a total show-off! Rob was in charge of the youth club. If Rob had been there, Adam certainly wouldn't have been standing on the table like that, but for some reason Rob was late that afternoon. The caretaker had let them in – and they'd found a note on the board: *Don't go crazy! I'll be half an hour late. Great surprise coming up! Rob.*

Martina had no idea what the great surprise might be, but she was sure it would be something good. Rob was always coming up with interesting things for them to do: trips to the beach, outings to sports events and concerts, visits to interactive museums. The summer holidays were never boring with Rob around to keep things buzzing.

'All hail the mighty Adam!' Martina called up to him with a laugh. 'We are not worthy!'

'True,' Adam said, grinning widely. 'Very true.'

'If Rob catches you up there, you'll find out who the *real* master is around here,' Sam chuckled.

Adam laughed. 'The Mighty Adam cares nothing for the likes of Rob!' he cried dramatically.

The doors swung open and Rob came in. Martina grinned mischievously and looked up at her friend. Since he had his back to the door, Adam hadn't seen Rob's arrival. Everyone else had, though.

'So what would you say if Rob *did* catch you?' Martina asked innocently. Everyone looked on, grinning. Adam was the only one who still hadn't noticed the tall, well-built twenty-one-year-old youth club leader as he walked slowly into the room with a wide smile on his face.

'What would I say?' wondered Adam. 'I'd say – bow down before me, Rob, for I am the true Ruler of this Youth Club!'

'That's what you'd say, is it?' said Rob.

Adam spun around with a marvellous look of shock and dismay on his face. He slipped, lost his footing and came bumping down on his backside.

Martina joined in the general laughter.

'Are you OK, *Mighty Adam*?' Rob asked. 'Looks like you bruised your mighty bottom there!'

Adam laughed. 'I'm fine,' he said. 'The Mighty Adam cares nothing for bruised bottoms.' He looked around at the grinning faces. 'I've been keeping this lot under control for you.'

'I just bet you have,' Rob said. 'And, by the way, if I catch you larking about up on that table again, I'm going to pull your legs off and knot them around your neck.' His voice was friendly, but everyone knew that the warning was serious, even if the threat wasn't.

'Don't worry, I'll do my celebrating at floor level from now on,' Adam said a little sheepishly. Then he gave Rob a wide smile. 'So, what's the big surprise?'

Rob raised his voice so that everyone could hear him. 'I've been in a meeting with the people who are organizing the summer carnival this year,' he boomed. 'And I've managed to arrange it so that Island Youth Club has its own float in the parade!'

There was a collective whoop of joy and excitement.

'That's so cool!' Martina exclaimed happily to Sam.

The Stowham City Summer Street Carnival was *the* great event of the summer. All the people taking part in the carnival parade would gather early on the first Saturday morning of August in Pelham Park. At ten o'clock sharp the parade would wind out of the park gates, down Fulsome Street, up Tibbs Road and off across the town centre in a long, colourful, noisy snake that would finish up right across the other side of town in Belair Gardens. In Belair there was always a funfair, stalls, food and an open-air music concert.

Plenty of summers, Martina had stood in the crowds that lined the streets. When she was little, she had perched on her dad's shoulders. More recently, she had stood with her friends, cheering the marching bands, acrobats and cheerleaders, applauding the great gaudy, fantastic floats as they trundled by like rainbows on wheels, waving up at the costumed people on the floats and wishing she could be up there herself.

'Rob, the carnival is only *two weeks* away!' someone called out.

'That's right,' Rob said. 'We have a fortnight to get everything ready.'

'Are we going to be able to do it all in time?' Martina asked.

'I think so,' Rob said. 'I didn't tell you about it, just in case it didn't come off, but I got wind of the fact that we might be offered a float several weeks ago. The theme of this year's carnival is "Myths and Legends of the World". Now, I've done some research and I've come up with an idea that I think you're going to like. If you just wait here for a few seconds I'll go and fetch some stuff.'

So saying, he waded through the crowd to the little room he used as an office. The murmur of voices began immediately, everyone eagerly discussing what kind of float they might have.

Rob soon returned, armed with a pile of papers. 'I've been talking to Arkstone's department store and they have kindly agreed to donate a heap of stuff to us,' he announced. 'We'll be getting a big van-load of fabrics and bric-a-brac from them. And Jepper's builders merchants are going to let us have a whole bunch of offcuts of timber and stuff with which we can make the frame of the float. The people at Garden World are loaning us one of their flat-back lorries to build the float on.' He handed out printouts. 'These are pictures of floats from last year's Rio Carnival – that's the biggest street carnival in the world.'

Martina grabbed a sheet. The float was totally amazing. It was designed like a huge fish, all in silver, green and blue, with shining scales and huge mirror-ball eyes. A young woman in a silver leotard was standing way up on the fish's head, smiling and waving as blue and silver ribbons streamed out behind her in the air.

'Now, obviously we can't expect to construct anything as elaborate or as complicated as the floats in these pictures,' Rob was saying. 'They took months to design and put together. But I want you to have a good look at the colours and designs and the ideas behind them, so we can do something totally spectacular that'll blow everyone's minds.' He raised his voice again. 'Are you all with me on this?'

'YESSSS!' everyone cheered.

'OK, then,' he continued. 'This will be *your* float, so you can shout me down if you don't like my idea, but the theme I've come up with is Mayan gods and goddesses.'

There was an immediate hubbub of excited voices. Martina didn't know very much about

Mayan mythology, but what she did know was intriguing and mysterious.

'I'm glad you all like the sound of it,' Rob said. 'I'm going to pin these pictures on the board. They'll give you a better idea of what I'm on about.'

He went over to the long pin-board and started pinning pages up there. 'It'll probably be easier for you all to see if most of you sit on the floor,' he suggested.

Everyone gathered around on the floor. Martina sat right at the front with Sam; she wanted to see exactly what Rob had in mind.

The board was soon filled with colourful pictures of male and female characters in bizarre costumes, and with distinctly odd, and sometimes quite monstrous, faces. Next to each picture was a written description of the god depicted.

'You can have a closer look at these later,' Rob said. 'These are the gods and goddesses of the Ancient Mayan people. Can anyone tell me where the Mayans lived?'

'Didn't they live in Mexico?' someone called out.

'That's right,' Rob said. 'They first arrived there about four and a half thousand years ago, but their empire was at its height around 250 AD. They're thought to have been the first people in the Americas to have used writing and to have come up with calendars. But the part of their culture that I find most interesting is their mythology. As you can see from the printouts, their gods and goddesses were a colourful bunch, and I suggest that we recreate one of their mythological stories for our float.'

'Did they sacrifice people, like the Aztecs did?' Sam asked.

'They did,' Rob replied. 'But they weren't quite as bloodthirsty as the Aztecs, and "sacrificing" a person didn't always mean killing them. The story I'd like us to recreate is one where Ah Puch – God of Death – came to earth. He was in a really bad mood because he didn't think the people were worshipping him as much as they should, and he decided to punish them by taking away the "Breath of Life". Can anyone guess what that meant?'

'He was going to suffocate them?' someone suggested.

'Got it in one!' said Rob. 'Ah Puch came to earth, intending to kill half of the Mayan people by taking the air right out of their lungs, and he nearly succeeded too. In fact, the Mayan king became so desperate that he offered his own life in place of the lives of his people – and you have to realize that the death of the king was far more significant than the deaths of even hundreds of ordinary people. Ah Puch agreed to the deal, and the king was sacrificed. But then the God of Death went back on the deal; he started to suffocate the Mayan people. But the other gods would not allow the king's sacrifice to be in vain. They stepped in and saved the people by for ever trapping Ah Puch in the storm wind that had always signalled his approach. So, in the end, the only one to die was the Mayan king.'

'I vote Sam is the king!' Adam shouted.

Sam laughed. 'I'd die in a much cooler way than you, anyhow,' he told his friend.

'We'll draw lots for who plays what role,' Rob said. 'That's the only fair way to do it. Some of you will be gods and goddesses, one of you will be the king, and the rest of you will be priests and dancers and ordinary Mayan people.' He pointed in turn to six of the most colourful pictures. 'These are the main Mayan gods that I think we should have in the parade. Each of them will need an elaborate costume, which I want you guys to design and make yourselves, and each of them will have their own dance to perform on the day. I've asked Caitlin Morris to come and work on the dance routines with us.'

Martina liked the sound of that. She'd been to some salsa classes that Caitlin had run. They'd been really good.

'Right, here are some pieces of paper,' Rob continued. 'I want each of you to write your name on a piece, fold it up and put it in the box in my office. Once everyone's name is in the box, we'll draw lots to see who gets to be what.'

'And Kukulkan, God of Earth, Fire, Water and Air, will be Barry Knowles,' Rob announced a little while later as he drew another slip of paper from the box.

'Excellent!' Barry called. 'All I've got to do now is learn how to say my name without tying my tongue in a knot!'

Rob had already picked several priests and ordinary townsfolk. Chac, God of Rain and Thunder, was Estelle. Yumil Kaxob, God of Maize, was Jake Hobart. Three of the gods still hadn't been picked. Rob dipped his hand into the box again.

'OK, Ix Chel will be . . . Martina Burrows!'

Martina gave a yell of delight. It was just the role she'd been hoping for. She looked at the picture of Ix Chel pinned to the board. The goddess was beautiful and her costume was every colour of the rainbow. Martina knew she'd have a great time coming up with a really fabulous costume, and she was already looking forward to working with Caitlin on a spectacular dance routine.

'Kinich Ahan, God of the Sun, will be Noel Greenhalf,' Rob's voice rang out again.

Sam still didn't have a role. 'I hope I don't have to be a god,' he whispered to Martina. 'There's no way I could go on a float, prancing around in front of people. I'd rather be an ordinary Mayan.'

The draw was down to the last few people now. Adam still didn't have a role, and neither did Sam.

The only god still unaccounted for was Ah Puch, God of Death. And the only other main role left unclaimed was that of the king. Looking around, Martina realized that only Sam's and Adam's names were left in the box. One of them was going to be the god of death; the other would be his royal sacrifice.

'Ah Puch will be performed by . . .' Rob unfolded

the slip of paper and smiled, 'the "Mighty" Adam!'

'Woohoo!' whooped Adam, jumping up and punching the air. He looked over at Sam. 'Sorry about this, King Sam, but it looks as if I'm going to have to sacrifice you.'

Sam smiled. 'As long as you do it humanely,' he joked.

'It's a deal!' Adam agreed.

Rob took the last piece of paper out of the box. 'I'm afraid he's right, Sam,' Rob said. 'You're the king. That means you get pride of place at the top of the float.'

'When do I get to slaughter him?' Adam asked.

'You don't,' Rob said. 'In our version everyone survives.'

'Awww,' Adam said miserably.

'OK, everyone,' Rob said. 'I want volunteers to help with the design and construction of the float. I've made a few preliminary plans and sketches, but I'm going to need plenty of help. And I'll need people here early tomorrow morning, ready for when the donated gear starts to arrive. And, people,' he raised his voice above the excited murmur, 'We've got less than two weeks to do this, so I don't want anyone goofing off. If we make this good, the council will probably let us have a float again next year, so I'm relying on you all to do your best.'

'I'm going to look Ix Chel up on the internet,' Martina said later as she and Sam walked home through the warm summer streets. 'Would you like to come over to my place and check it out with me?'

'OK, sounds cool,' Sam said. 'Rob's pictures were really good, but we might find some more stuff for the costumes and some extra ideas for the float.'

They heard running footsteps behind them, and a second later Adam was upon them, his arms around their necks as he butted in between them.

'Chill out, guys,' he said, grinning widely. 'It's only me, God of *Death*!'

Sam laughed and the three friends walked on together for a while, chatting excitedly about the youth club float, until they came to the corner where Adam had to turn off to go home.

'So, what are you two doing this evening?' Adam asked as they stood on the street corner.

'We're going over to my place to look up the Mayan gods on the internet,' Martina said. 'Want to come?'

'I can't,' Adam said. 'I told Dad I'd help him out in the garden this evening. He's putting up some wire mesh to try and stop the rooks from the park eating his seedlings. Dad thinks they're pretty cool when they're in the trees, but when they're eating his vegetables, not so much!' Adam's garden backed on to Pelham Park where a row of tall elm trees made a home for a whole community of rooks. 'Still, I might do some research of my own on the computer once that's done.' He walked off. 'See you tomorrow, guys. And don't be late – or the God of Death may have to kill you!'

* * *

There turned out to be plenty of information online about the Mayan people and their gods. Martina and Sam sat side by side at the computer in the dining-room, while her parents watched a wildlife documentary in the lounge.

Martina made scribbled notes to help her remember the things she found particularly interesting. She was especially taken with an illustration of Ix Chel, dressed in her colourful robes and wearing a curved headdress of blue, yellow and red, which had long green quills rising out of it like slender leaves.

' "Ix Chel's name means Lady Rainbow",' Martina read. 'She's the goddess of the moon and of weaving and of childbirth.' She gazed at the bright colours of the costume in the picture. 'I'm going to wear something just like that,' she told Sam, beginning to make a rough sketch of the costume.

While she was busy with this, she saw that Sam

was checking out a site concerning Ah Puch, God of Death.

'This site's got some great stuff on it,' he told her. 'I can't wait to show Adam. Apparently, Ah Puch is generally depicted as a skeleton with big, empty eye sockets.' He bit his lip thoughtfully. 'We could paint Adam's face white, like a skull, and draw teeth on his lips, and paint his eye sockets with black face paint. He'll look amazing! And it says here that his "adornments" – I suppose that means clothes – are mostly made of bones and decomposing stuff and bells. Oh, and he's sometimes shown with the head of an owl.'

'I can't see Adam wanting the head of an *owl*,' Martina said. 'But I think he'd like being a skeleton.'

'It says he travels on a storm wind, and that a great black bird of ill omen flies ahead to herald his approach,' Sam told her.

Martina chuckled. 'It's a pity those rooks in the park at the end of his garden can't be trained,' she said. 'Adam could use one of them as his "black bird of ill omen".'

' "And Ah Puch has a black mark in the shape of a flying bird on his forehead",' Sam read. He looked at Martina. 'We could put that on Adam's skull-forehead,' he said. 'I can't wait to tell him all this stuff. He'll love it.'

Eventually, Sam had to head for home, leaving Martina sketching out different ideas for her costume as Lady Rainbow.

Martina had a few chores around the house to do before she could go to the youth club the next day, so it was the afternoon before she set off with a bundle of drawings under her arm.

She arrived to find some people sorting through big cardboard boxes of stuff from the department store and others unloading lengths of timber and hardboard from a Jepper's van under Rob's guidance.

The lorry from the garden centre had also

arrived. It was stationed in the car park beside the building, waiting to be made to look spectacular!

Martina found Adam and Sam deep in conversation about Ah Puch. They both looked up as she arrived. Sam's face was glowing with excitement.

'After I left you, I went online again at home,' he told her eagerly. 'I was just telling Adam. I looked on eBay and found a genuine Ah Puch face-mask for sale.' He grinned. 'I even talked my dad into putting in a bid for it!'

Martina stared at him. 'A *genuine* face-mask?' she asked, sitting down next to her friends. 'Can it really be *genuine*?'

'Well, it would have to be hundreds of years old,' Sam said, showing her a printout of the eBay page, 'so I don't know about that, but I guess it's possible.'

Martina peered at the pictures of the wooden mask. 'Ewww!' she exclaimed. It wasn't the simple depiction of a skull that she had been expecting.

Instead it was like the head of a corpse, with flesh rotting off the bones in strips and chunks. The vivid colours seemed slightly faded by time, but the dark reds, sickly yellows and rotting greens still showed clearly against the white of the bones.

'It's got a really low start price,' Sam went on. 'And the auction ends today. Dad's already put a bid in. And the really great thing is that the guy selling it only lives a half-hour drive from us. Dad says he'll go and pick it up if we win.'

'I hope you do,' Adam said, grinning at the gruesome mask. 'The ideas you had for painting my face are good, but a mask like this would be way cool!'

Martina looked at the starting price: it was very low. 'I seriously doubt that it's going to be genuine,' she said. 'Not at that price! Besides, if it was real, surely it would be in a museum.'

'I don't care if it's genuine or not,' Adam said. 'It looks brilliant!'

'It looks disgusting!' Martina laughed. She eyed

the picture again. 'But there's one good thing,' she added, grinning at Adam. 'At least it'll hide your face!'

Sam laughed and Adam pretended to slap her.

'I've been telling Adam some of our ideas for his costume,' Sam said eagerly.

'They're pretty good,' Adam said. 'And they've given me an idea for something that's going to look totally amazing. I'm going to go with the skeleton look, OK, but I'm going to be wearing a big cloak of black feathers. It'll look awesome!'

'Where will you get all the feathers from?' Martina asked.

'That's easy,' Adam said. 'I'll nip over the back fence and pick them up in the park. Those rooks are always shedding feathers. There are probably dozens of them lying about down there.'

Rob's head appeared around the door. 'Come on, guys. There's no time to sit around chatting. Let's get to work!'

They jumped up enthusiastically and followed

him out to help with a second delivery of fabrics, cans of paint, brushes and plenty of other bits and pieces from the department store. Martina spotted some marvellous stuff, including bales of sparkling, iridescent cloth and some pieces of fake fur.

It took a couple of hours to get everything organized. Then they had a break while Rob sat on the side of the lorry and explained his ideas for the float.

'I want to make a miniature version of the kind of world in which the Mayans lived,' he said. 'So, most importantly, we need to construct a big square pyramid in the middle of the truck.'

'Could it be a stepped pyramid rather than a smooth one?' Sam suggested. 'That way we can have people standing on each level.'

'Great idea!' Rob said. 'And right at the top of the pyramid, we can have a golden throne for Sam to sit on. He's going to be the centre of attention since he's the sacrifice.'

'We found some websites on the internet last

night,' Martina said. 'The Mayan gods and goddesses were all involved with nature—'

'So maybe we could decorate the pyramid with trees and flowers,' Sam broke in animatedly. 'Like a jungle.'

'Yes, marvellous,' Rob agreed. 'That's perfect.'

'We could paint the pyramid so it looks like a mountain,' Sam continued thoughtfully. 'And we could use some of that thin white netting material the department store sent us to create waterfalls. If we attach it at the top of the pyramid and let it hang down the sides it would look great!'

'Excellent thinking, Sam,' Rob said. 'Now, I need a few volunteers to help me make the frame of the pyramid. It'll have to be good and strong, and the council health and safety people will want to check it to make sure it's solid enough for you lot to clamber over.'

Martina knew that Rob wouldn't have any problem making the pyramid frame safe. He was a skilled carpenter and he'd made plenty of things that they used in the club, including the table-tennis table that Adam had been fooling about on yesterday.

Work began again, and Martina dived into the heaps of cloth, picking out the brightest and most colourful pieces for her costume. Once she had all the colours she wanted, she was going to take them home and ask her mum to help her sew them into rainbow robes that would dazzle everyone!

Time flew that afternoon. By the early evening, the fabrics had been sorted out into greens and browns for the jungle, and people had already begun to glue and staple lengths on to wooden and cardboard backings, making trees and bushes. Others were busy painting animals on to cardboard sheets – jaguars, coyotes, snakes, scorpions and vultures soon populated the youth club.

And Rob and his small band of woodworkers were making swift progress. All afternoon there had been the noise of sawing and drilling and hammering, and by early evening the basic frame for the first level of the pyramid was finished and secured in place on the back of the lorry.

Coming out from the club rooms, Martina gazed up into the clear blue evening sky. She hoped the weather would continue fine so that they could get the float finished. Rob had a huge tarpaulin to hand so that the float could be covered at night and in case of rain, but the weather forecast was good.

Martina and Adam were just handing a long piece of timber up to Rob and Sam on the back of the lorry, when Sam's mobile beeped.

He took the phone out of his pocket. 'It's a text from Dad,' he said, looking at it. Then he let out a yell of excitement. 'We did it! We got the mask!' He scrolled down the message. 'Dad has arranged to go over and pick it up on his way home from work this evening.'

'Brilliant!' Adam yelled up to him. 'Bring it in tomorrow. I want to try it on.'

'You bet!' Sam replied.

Martina felt a shiver of excitement – the way things were shaping up, they were going to create the most thrilling carnival float Stowham had ever seen!

Martina spent most of the evening explaining to her mum what she wanted her costume to look like. She told her about an idea she'd had of tying coloured ribbons to her wrists so that they'd flutter as she moved. She also wanted to cover her face, arms and hands with glitter, and carry a pouch of silver glitter so that she could throw handfuls of it in the air as she danced. She wanted it to look like she was spilling silvery drops of moonlight as she moved.

They made paper templates of the costume and laid them out on the floor of the lounge, getting right in the way of her dad as he tried to watch the football. Then they pinned the cloth to each piece of paper until they had everything worked out.

Finally they cut all the pieces. Tomorrow night, her mum promised to get the sewing-machine out and start stitching the robes together.

Martina made sure she arrived early at the club the next day. Even so, she found Adam and Sam already there. They were on their own in the hallway that led to the club rooms, so involved in whatever they were talking about that they didn't even notice Martina as she approached.

Drawing closer, she saw that they were bent over the Ah Puch mask that Sam had got. They were deep in conversation, but, unusually, Sam was doing all the talking while Adam listened patiently, nodding every now and then in agreement.

'Hi, guys,' she said. Sam looked at her and grinned, and Martina noticed a strange mark on his forehead. 'What have you done to your face?' she asked. The sore-looking scratch ran down his forehead above his right eye.

'I got a splinter,' Sam said. 'From this!' He lifted up the ugly wooden mask.

In real life the hideous corpse-head looked even more revolting than it had in the pictures Martina had seen yesterday. *But then*, she thought, *what would you expect the God of Death to look like?* She had to admit that it was impressive.

'I tried it on last night when Dad brought it home,' Sam told her. He gestured towards the red scratch. 'That's where I got the splinter from. It was quite rough inside, but Dad's sanded it down now so it's totally safe.' He turned the mask to show her the inner face. 'See?' he said. 'There's a leather strap attached to the sides. It goes around your head and you can tighten it with the buckle, so it stays on without you having to hold it.'

Martina eyed the leather strap. 'There's no way that strap is genuine,' she said. 'The leather would have rotted away.'

'The guy who was selling it said he put the strap on himself,' Sam told her. 'But he told my dad that as far as he knows the mask is genuine. Apparently, he inherited it from an elderly relative who used to collect Ancient Mayan stuff.' He grinned. 'The guy's wife hated it,' he continued. 'She thought it was evil, and told him to get it out of the house, so he put it on eBay.'

'It certainly looks real enough,' Martina agreed. She looked at Adam. He was standing there, oddly quiet, staring at the mask with an unusually thoughtful expression on his face. 'Have you tried it on yet?' she asked him.

He stared at her as if she'd snapped him out of a trance. 'No, not yet,' he replied.

'What are you waiting for?' Martina asked.

'I'm not sure I want to right now,' Adam said hesitantly.

'Oh, put the mask on,' Sam snapped. 'Put it on *now*.'

Adam took the mask from Sam and held it up to his face. Sam tightened the strap around Adam's head. 'Is that OK?' he asked.

'Fine,' Adam replied. He turned to face Martina. 'How do I look?'

Martina had to suppress a shudder as she looked at the mask. It had been horrible enough before, but now, with Adam's light-blue eyes peering out from the black eye sockets, it seemed almost alive. Well, as alive as something with the appearance of having just crawled out of a grave could ever look!

'Give us a dance,' Sam said.

Adam began to stalk around the hallway, his head tilted imperiously upwards, his arms stretched out and his fingers curled like claws. 'You are my slaves!' he growled in a guttural, threatening voice. 'Bow to my will.'

'Hey, not bad,' Martina declared.

Adam stalked towards her, stamping his feet in a slow rhythm.

'Creepy God of Death,' she said with a laugh. 'Go and show the others!'

Adam lunged for her, and with a shiver she jumped back to avoid his outstretched hands.

'Go and dance outside,' Sam grinned at Adam. 'They'll all want to see you.'

With a grunt of agreement, Adam turned on his heel and swept along the hallway to the door.

Martina and Sam followed him as he stepped out into the open. A dozen or more people were out there, working on the float. Adam went stamping towards them. A couple of the girls squealed at the sight of the mask. Martina didn't blame them – even in broad daylight it looked pretty gruesome.

Rob stood up on the lorry, a hammer in his hand, grinning as Adam sent the girls running. 'Hey, Adam,' he called down. 'I thought you were going to be wearing a mask.' He laughed as the ugly face stared up at him and Adam emitted an eerie howl. 'Oh, sorry, you *are* wearing one,' Rob said.

Adam pointed a threatening finger up at Rob. 'You will regret mocking Ah Puch,' he snarled. 'None may defy the God of Death!'

Martina looked at Sam. 'He's really getting into it, isn't he?' she said.

Sam smiled. 'That's Adam for you,' he said. 'Hey, Adam!' he called. 'You can take it off now!'

Adam turned and pulled the mask off. Underneath, his face was quite red and sweaty. 'How was I?' he asked.

'Brilliant!' Martina said, clapping. 'Absolutely brilliant!'

There was an air of excitement in the club rooms all the rest of the day. Martina and Sam spent some time helping to cut up sheets of green card into leaf-shapes and then taping the leaves on to wire frames that had been twisted, bent and covered with layers of papier-mâché so that they looked like jungle trees.

Other people were making papier-mâché rocks and boulders, while more were cutting strips of green and brown and yellow fabric, stitching them together and twisting them around and around so that they looked like jungle lianas.

Every now and then Rob would do the rounds,

checking on how things were going and making useful suggestions, but most of his time was spent building the slowly rising wooden frame of the pyramid.

It was some hours later that Martina noticed that the God of Death was missing.

'Have you seen Adam?' she asked Sam, who was tacking a painted hardboard lion on to a wooden frame so that it would stand up on its own.

'Not for a while,' Sam replied. 'Why?'

Martina shrugged. 'I just wondered where he was.' Now she came to think about it, she hadn't seen or heard any sign of Adam for some time. *What's he up to?* she wondered. It wasn't like him to be missing for so long. She decided to go and find out.

She located him quite quickly. He was out in the small kitchen area, sitting all alone on the worktop alongside the sink, staring at the mask that was lying face up on his knees.

'What are you doing in here?' Martina asked.

He jumped as if she'd startled him. 'Nothing,' he replied, sliding down off the worktop. 'Did you want me for something?'

'Nothing in particular,' Martina told him. 'I just wondered where you were.'

'I was here,' Adam said flatly.

'I can see that.' She frowned at him. 'Why?'

He gave her a curious, lopsided grin. 'I was just looking at this,' he said. He held the mask up, the hideous face towards her. 'Pretty, isn't he?'

Martina winced. 'Yes, lovely,' she said.

Adam gave her a long, thoughtful look. 'He's the God of Death, you know,' he said, and he gave her that peculiar lopsided grin again. It was such an odd kind of grin – nothing like Adam's usual toothy smile. It almost looked, well, *sad*, as if there was something bothering him. Martina began to wonder if he was having problems at home.

'Uh, yes, I know he is,' she said, peering closely at Adam's face. 'Are you OK?'

He nodded. 'Yes, I'm fine.' He tucked the mask

under his arm and walked out past her. She heard him whistling shrilly between his teeth as he walked off, and the discordant sound set her teeth on edge.

'Hey,' she called after him. 'I didn't know you couldn't whistle!'

She waited for the typical, quick-fire Adam Dalston retort. But he didn't say a word.

Now that *really is odd*, Martina thought.

Adam was even less like his usual self the following day. He arrived at the club with a stack of books under one arm and a green garden sack under the other. Without saying 'hi' to anyone, he went off into a corner of the main room, put the books down on a chair and opened the green bag.

Martina watched as Adam took a large swathe of black cloth out of the bag and spread it out on a table. Then he produced a needle and some black thread. He ignored everyone around him completely.

At last, Martina could stand it no longer. She walked over to find out why Adam wasn't talking to anyone.

'Hi, Adam,' she said. 'Is that your costume?'

'Yes,' he replied coldly, without even looking at her.

'You didn't say hello when you arrived,' Martina tried.

'Hello,' he said flatly.

'*Adam!*' Martina exclaimed.

'I'm busy,' he replied, and he reached down into the bag and pulled out a big handful of black feathers.

'Did you get those from the park?' she asked, determined to get Adam talking, in the hope that he'd open up to her and give her a clue as to what was wrong.

'Yes.' He threaded the needle and placed one of the long feathers on the cloth.

'Did you get enough for the whole cloak?' Martina asked.

'No.'

'So, what are you going to do about the rest?'

'I'll think of something,' Adam muttered, sewing on the feather. He stared at his handiwork for a few moments, then nodded in apparent satisfaction and placed a second feather beside the first.

'You've got quite a job on your hands there,' Martina said. 'Want any help?'

'No. I'm fine.'

She paused, looking at the top of Adam's lowered head. 'Are you OK?' she asked after a few moments.

'Yes.'

She frowned. 'Got any good jokes?'

'No. I'm busy. Go away.'

Martina gave him a concerned look. 'OK,' she sighed. 'I will. But you're going to have to talk to me eventually. I'm not stupid, Adam, and I know there's something wrong with you.'

For the first time, he looked up at her, and his eyes were oddly empty. 'There's nothing wrong with me at all,' he said coolly.

She frowned. 'If you say so.' And, with that, she left him to it.

Martina went to talk to Sam. He was his usual self, thank goodness, except that he now had a plaster on his forehead covering the spot where he'd been stabbed by the splinter from the mask.

'Is it painful?' Martina asked, pointing at the plaster.

'Nope,' he said. 'My mum's just being paranoid. She's afraid it might get infected.'

Martina glanced over to the quiet corner where Adam was working on his cloak. 'Adam's really acting strangely today,' she said. 'He hardly said a word to me just now.'

'I expect he's just concentrating on his costume,' Sam suggested.

'But it's not like him. Can't you go and talk to him?' Martina asked.

Sam looked at her. 'And say what? If he doesn't feel like talking, then I think we should leave him alone.'

'Typical boy!' Martina said in exasperation. 'He's been down ever since yesterday. Don't you care?'

Sam sighed. 'Look, if I was feeling fed up about something, the last thing I'd want is for people to keep on asking about it. Let him be.'

Martina shook her head. 'You're hopeless!' she said.

It was much later when Martina went over to Adam again. The long black cloak had come a long way since she'd last looked. Adam had made vertical cuts up the cloak so that it hung in wide strips. The bottom half of each strip was now covered in black feathers, the green bag was empty on the floor and Adam was engrossed in one of his books. The rest were scattered on the table.

Peering over his shoulder, Martina realized that the books were all textbooks and encyclopaedias. Those that weren't closed lay open on pages of information about the Mayan gods – especially Ah Puch.

'Where did you get all these books?' Martina asked in amazement; it wasn't like Adam to take anything this seriously.

'The library,' Adam replied, without looking up from his page.

'I'm surprised you knew where it was,' Martina teased, waiting for a snappy response.

'Yates Street,' Adam stated dismissively.

'Yes, *I* know where it is, I just meant . . . Oh, skip it,' Martina sighed. 'Hey, the cloak is coming on nicely. Try it on. Let's see how it looks.'

'Not yet,' Adam said. 'It's not finished.'

'Fair enough.' She smiled encouragingly. 'Listen, if something's bothering you, Adam, you know you can always talk to me, don't you? And I promise I won't say a word to anyone else if you don't want me to. My mum always says, a problem shared is—'

Adam looked up at her impatiently, and Martina was surprised by how pale he was. 'Why are you interrupting me?' he asked sharply. 'Can't you see I'm trying to read?'

She grinned hopefully. 'It's a bit late for you to start trying at your age,' she joked.

Adam just stared blankly at her for a moment and then turned back to his book.

'Oh, I give up,' Martina muttered. *I've done all I can*, she thought. *If he doesn't want to talk to me, I can't make him!*

'Perhaps he's just getting into character,' Sam suggested when Martina brought up the subject of Adam's bad mood again later. 'I was reading about it in a magazine the other day. Some actors will stay in character even when they're not actually performing. Apparently it helps them to really get into the role. Like, if they're a teacher or a doctor, they'll spend all day behaving like a teacher or a doctor.'

Martina eyed him uncertainly. 'And if they were playing the God of Death, they'd act that way all day?' she asked dubiously.

'Exactly,' Sam confirmed.

'And you think that's what Adam's doing – really getting into the role of Ah Puch?' She glanced over at Adam, who was still absorbed in his Mayan mythology books. *Maybe Sam's right*, she thought. *Maybe that* is *what Adam's doing*.

'Let's hope he doesn't take it too far on the day,' she said, grinning at Sam, 'or I wouldn't fancy being the royal sacrifice on our float!'

She was only kidding, of course, but she was getting freaked out by the quiet, grumpy Adam that had replaced her mischievous, fun-loving friend. Still, if Sam was right, then Adam would be back to his normal self as soon as the carnival was over. Martina just hoped she could cope with sharing the youth club with Ah Puch till then!

Later that afternoon, Caitlin Morris came down to see them for the first time.

Rob gathered everyone together. 'Here's the thing,' he announced. 'We're going great guns with the float, and I can see you're all getting on very well with your costumes, so I thought maybe it was time for us to think about the choreography. If you remember, I told you that the six main gods would each have their own dance, but all the rest of you will need to learn a few dance steps, too. That's why I've asked Caitlin to come down and help with our routines.'

Caitlin stepped forward. 'Hi there, everyone,' she said. 'Now, I think a really good way for you all to get into the right frame of mind for this is if you put your costumes on. I know the costumes aren't finished yet, but I can see that most of you have something you can wear, so what say you all get dressed up, and then we'll get things rolling?'

Everybody was excited at the prospect of trying out their half-finished costumes. It took a few minutes for them all to get dressed up, during which time Martina described her costume to Caitlin: the coloured robes, the glitter, the flowing ribbons.

'But it's at home right now,' Martina explained.

'My mum is going to sew the pieces together tonight.'

'That's great, Martina,' Caitlin said. 'Bring it in tomorrow and you can show me any dance ideas you've had – knowing you, they'll be really good.'

'OK,' Martina said happily. She was distracted by a dark movement at the corner of her vision. She turned to look and had to stifle a yelp of shock. A gruesome figure stood by her side, his face covered by the Ah Puch mask, his body swathed in a black cloak.

'Adam!' Martina gasped, clutching her chest. 'Don't sneak up on me, especially not when you're dressed like that!'

'I am God of Death,' growled Adam, pointing a finger at her. 'Mortals beware my wrath!'

'Yeah, right,' Martina said. 'For your information, I'm the goddess Ix Chel, so go frighten someone else.'

Sam appeared. 'Of course, he'll look more

impressive on the day, won't you, Ah Puch?' he remarked.

The heavy mask nodded.

'He'll be dressed in a skeleton suit and there'll be a lot more feathers,' Sam explained to Caitlin.

'Very impressive,' Caitlin replied.

'You will be able to get more feathers, won't you?' Sam asked Adam.

'Yes,' Adam agreed quietly.

'Have you worked out your dance yet, Adam?' Caitlin asked.

Adam stared at her but didn't reply.

'Go on, show her your dance,' Sam said encouragingly.

Adam began the imperious stalking, stamping dance that he had performed earlier – except that now it seemed to Martina that Adam had made the whole thing much more sinister and scary. He let out fierce shouts and howls as he leaped and spun, his arms outstretched and his fingers bent like claws.

A few people laughed as he leaped towards

them, but plenty more drew back uneasily.

Martina turned to say something to Sam, but he'd gone. She looked around, and saw him sitting quietly on a table at the back of the room, watching Adam with a deep frown on his face. Martina wondered if Sam was finally beginning to notice the changes in Adam that had been worrying her.

'Wow!' Caitlin called. 'That's a really great dance, Adam. I really don't think we're going to have to change that at all, so let me see if the other gods have come up with any dance moves yet.'

But Adam didn't quit his creepy dance. If anything, it grew more intense, his cloak spreading out behind him as he whirled menacingly about the room.

A shiver went down Martina's spine as she watched him. He was certainly very convincing as a God of Death. She could easily believe that there was something evil and malicious hidden away under that mask.

She moved over to join Sam.

'Adam, that's enough, thanks,' Caitlin called. 'Give someone else a chance. Come on!'

Martina gazed into Sam's face. He was staring at Adam as though he was completely mesmerized by him.

'Is it just me, or do you think Adam's getting a bit too caught up in his role?' she asked. She waved her hand in front of Sam's face. 'Hey! Hello-o-o! Anyone home?'

Sam blinked at her. 'Oh, sorry,' he said. 'What did you say?'

'I said I think Adam's getting a bit carried away,' Martina repeated. 'Caitlin's asked him to stop twice now, and he won't!'

'He *has* stopped,' Sam said.

Martina looked over her shoulder. Sure enough, Adam had now taken off the mask and was sitting cross-legged on the floor against the wall. The half-finished cloak was bundled up beside him with the mask. He looked completely exhausted.

Caitlin was tutoring a few priests in a simple dance routine and no one was taking any notice of Adam any more.

'He looks ill,' Martina said. Adam's face was red and sweaty, and his hair was sticking to his forehead. 'Do you think there's something wrong with him?' she went on. 'You know, like flu or something? That might explain why he's been so off lately.'

Sam shrugged. 'Could be,' he said. 'But it must have been hot dancing around in that cloak and mask. That could be why he's red and sweaty.'

Martina frowned. 'Maybe,' she said uneasily. 'But if he's not ill, then I'm beginning to think he's taking this whole thing way too seriously.'

That night, Martina had some very strange and unpleasant dreams about Ah Puch. In the worst one, she approached Adam in his costume and took the mask off his face, only to find a leering fleshless skull beneath – a skull with evil red eyes in hollow black eye sockets. That one woke her up and left her feeling so creeped-out that she switched her bedside light on.

The nightmare faded away quickly as she lay gazing at the beautiful rainbow gown that hung on her wardrobe door. Between them, she and her mother had managed to sew the whole thing together that evening. It was perfect, exactly as Martina had imagined it – a long, flowing dress of every imaginable colour. And her mum had managed to find some shining ribbons for her wrists and hair. Martina couldn't wait for everyone at the club to see it, and she was eager to show Caitlin the dance routine she had worked out. With any luck, Lady Rainbow was going to be the star of the show!

After a few minutes, she switched the light off again and pulled the covers up over her head. The horrible image of the skull had faded, but the thing that stopped her from getting straight back to sleep was the odd feeling that Adam had *changed* in the past few days. Sam's suggestion that Adam was simply getting into character was all very well, but the difference was so extreme that it was almost as if Adam's own personality was being crushed under . . . under *what*? Martina asked herself. Under the personality of the Mayan God of Death? Hardly! Martina couldn't believe *that* for a single second, but all the same, she thought that Adam should tone his performance down. It was getting a bit too scary.

Martina decided to drop by Adam's house on the way to the youth club the following morning. She was missing the *real* Adam, and she wanted to talk to him away from the club. It wasn't far out of her way, and it was a clear bright morning as she headed along his street with her Ix Chel gown folded carefully in a carrier bag. As she walked up the front path, she heard the cawing of birds from beyond the rooftops of the terraced houses.

She paused, staring up as a whole flock of black

birds went wheeling up into the sky, cawing noisily. Martina recognized the birds – they were the rooks that nested high in the trees just beyond the bottom of Adam's garden. The way they were wheeling and calling, it seemed as if something had upset them. Perhaps a cat had disturbed them, or a fox. Whatever it was, Martina could see that the birds were annoyed and agitated as she pressed the doorbell.

Adam's mum answered the door. She told Martina that Adam was out in the garden and sent her through to find him.

Martina wandered down the long, narrow garden. There was no sign of Adam, and Martina guessed that he had climbed over the fence into the park to find some more feathers. That would explain why the rooks were still circling watchfully in the sky above the tall trees.

A compost maker stood up against the fence. Martina knew that it was Adam's usual way of getting quickly into the park. She climbed up on to it to look over the fence, and gave a yelp of surprise as Adam's face popped up right in front of her.

'Hello,' he said. 'Here, help me with this.' He passed a green garden sack over to her. It was bulky, but not heavy.

'What's in here?' Martina asked. 'More feathers?'

'Got it in one,' Adam said, boosting himself up on to the top of the fence. He sat astride it for a moment, then jumped easily down into the garden.

'I think you've upset the birds,' Martina remarked.

'They'll get over it,' Adam said carelessly.

Martina jumped down. As she did so, she felt something heavier than feathers bump about in the sack. 'What else have you got in here?' she asked, opening the mouth of the sack. 'It isn't only feathers.'

'You don't want to look in there,' Adam said. 'I know how squeamish girls are about that kind of thing.'

Martina gave him a hard look, then peered into

the sack. There were plenty of black feathers in there, but she saw something else as well, half buried in the feathers, she could make out the body of a black bird.

'Ewww!' she cried out, dropping the sack. 'There's a dead bird in there!'

'Yes,' Adam said lightly. 'I think a cat must have got it.'

'And you picked it up?' Martina said. 'That's disgusting. You should just bury it, right now!'

Adam looked at her. 'I was going to use its wing feathers.' He shrugged. 'But I'll bury it instead, if it freaks you out.'

'Of course it does!' Martina exclaimed. *And, usually, it would freak you out too*, she thought, remembering how Adam was normally quite fond of the rooks. She looked at her friend. 'Listen,' she said. 'I think you need to chill out a bit with all this Ah Puch business. People are going to think you've gone crazy otherwise.'

'Oh, don't be so lame,' Adam said with a grin. 'I'm

playing the God of Death, for heaven's sake. I'm supposed to be evil and scary.'

'Not all the time!' Martina exclaimed.

Adam laughed, but it sounded forced and unnatural.

'Just tone it down a little,' she said. 'Stop trying to creep people out.'

He looked at her. 'You're the one who's gone crazy,' he said. 'It's a laugh, that's all. Listen, I've got a few things to do here before I go to the club. You go on ahead and I'll see you there later.'

'OK,' Martina said. She pointed to the sack. 'But make sure you bury that poor bird.'

He nodded. 'Whatever you say.'

Martina walked away up the garden. *As soon as I get to the club, I'm going to have another talk with Sam,* she thought as she left the house. *Adam is seriously losing it!*

She found Sam busily painting a sheet of plywood with tall spikes of grass.

'Does this look like the kind of grass you'd get in a jungle?' he asked her, leaning back and appraising his work so far.

'Yes, it looks great,' Martina replied distractedly. She knelt down beside him. 'Hey, Sam, I dropped by at Adam's place on the way here,' she said. 'He'd been collecting feathers.' She lowered her voice. 'And there was a dead bird in the bag! He was going to pull its feathers out for his cloak.' She looked at Sam. 'How creepy is that?'

Sam looked at her. 'A dead bird?'

Martina nodded.

'Weird!' Sam said, frowning.

'He thought it was OK and that I was just being squeamish,' Martina said. 'I made him promise to bury it, you see.'

Sam stirred his paint-brush in the jar of greenish water for a few moments, then looked at Martina. 'Did he have his catapult with him?' he asked.

'I don't know, I didn't really look,' Martina replied. 'Why?'

'I went round to his place last night, and he was out in the garden firing his catapult at Coke cans,' Sam said. 'I just wondered if he still had it with him when you saw him.'

Martina suddenly realized what Sam was getting at. 'You don't think he killed the bird with the catapult, do you?' she gasped.

'He's a very good shot,' Sam said thoughtfully. 'I expect he could hit a bird if he tried.'

'But he *wouldn't*,' Martina said.

'No, I'm sure he wouldn't,' Sam agreed. 'Forget I mentioned it. A cat probably got it, that's all.'

Martina chewed her lip. 'But what if he *did*?' she whispered uncertainly. 'What if he needed more feathers than he could find on the ground?' She stared at Sam in alarm. 'What if he's killing birds to make his costume?'

The final few days that led up to the carnival were a whirl of activity at the club. Despite Adam's change of behaviour, Martina was totally caught up in the excitement of the preparations. She could hardly wait to get there in the morning, and sometimes she'd still be rushing around in the late afternoon: putting the finishing touches to the float, organizing dance routines, helping with other people's costumes and so on.

Adam was still insisting on being Ah Puch pretty much 24/7. Martina did her best to ignore him, but she could tell that everyone was getting fed up with his bad moods now. There was almost a fight one afternoon when they were rehearsing the dramatic Stealing of the Breath of Life Dance, which involved the entire cast. Everyone around Ah Puch had to pretend to be suffocating and dying because of his evil curse. Adam lost his temper and really yelled at a couple of people for getting some of the steps wrong. Peter, the high priest, yelled back, and it looked like they were going to have a serious face-off, until Rob intervened and managed to cool the whole thing down. But Martina could tell that even easy-going

Rob was running out of patience with Adam's behaviour.

One thing that Adam refused to do was show people his full costume. He'd put on the mask and cloak to rehearse his dance, but underneath the black-feathered cloak, he just wore his usual jeans and T-shirt. He told Martina it was because he wanted people to be really shocked when they saw him in his full Death God role.

In the end, people started to avoid Adam whether he was in his mask and cloak or not. It struck Martina that if Adam was planning to freak everyone out, it was working a little too well. *In fact*, she thought, *he's lucky he hasn't been thrown out of the club once and for all.*

The Saturday of the carnival dawned bright and sunny. The streets were thronged with people eager to see the parade.

At ten in the morning, the long snake of the parade gradually began to stream out of Pelham

Park and thread its way through the crowded streets.

Standing with the others on the youth club float as it drove slowly along Tibbs Road, Martina gazed around happily. What a show! There was a marching band in uniform, headed by a cheerleading squad and drum majorettes expertly twirling their batons. There were tumblers, clowns and dancers. And the noise was almost overwhelming. The constant cheering of the crowd mixed with the clashing sounds of all the different kinds of music: the brass and drums of the marching bands, sound systems blasting out hip-hop and rap, and a steel band playing from one of the floats.

The floats themselves were spectacular. The one directly in front of Martina was all to do with Druids. They had built a replica of Stonehenge on the back of the lorry, and people in white robes were dancing in and out of the stones. Behind the youth club float another was dedicated to the Norse gods. It was decorated to look like a Viking longship and filled with people in warrior clothes and horned helmets. And behind that one was a lovely float, like a huge yellow and red butterfly, depicting a story from ancient Chinese mythology.

But wonderful as all the other floats were, Martina thought theirs was the best. It looked magnificent, the square pyramid-mountain rising up tier upon tier, festooned with trees and lianas and tumbling white-net waterfalls, not to mention the bright nodding blooms and tall exotic grasses where jungle animals lurked. On every step, brightly-robed priests and farmers and townsfolk stood and waved. And at the very top, six metres from the ground, Sam sat on his golden throne, dressed all in gold and silver as the king who would sacrifice his blood for his people! The only thing that seemed out of place, from Martina's point of view, was the sticking plaster on Sam's forehead where he had got the splinter. Still, it was skin-coloured and it didn't really show, especially not from a distance.

Martina danced along the side of the float in her crescent-shaped headdress and rainbow robes, loving the way the ribbons rippled through the air as she moved. Her mother had helped her with the glitter that flashed from her forehead and cheeks, and every now and then she would reach into the pouch at her waist and toss a sparkling cascade of silver glitter out over the crowds.

Clearly the crowd thought the youth club float looked fantastic as well, because Martina was aware of the rising tide of cheers and applause that moved through the spectators as their float passed by. And Martina had to hand it to him; in his own way, Adam was very nearly stealing the show! His full Ah Puch costume was stunning. He was dressed all in black, with skeleton bones painted on his trousers and shirt, and with what looked like real bones hanging from thongs around his waist and arms.

As he danced, surrounded by his priests, Ah Puch's huge feathered cloak billowed around him so that it almost looked as if he had great black wings. And he had done something to his hands as well – Martina couldn't quite see what, but his fingers really did look like the claws of some deadly bird of prey as he snatched at the air. But it was the mask that really completed the illusion. As Adam whirled and spun, it almost seemed to Martina that the gruesome mask had come to life.

And then something rather strange happened. As she danced, Martina spotted a small black shape moving across the sky. She didn't think much of it at first, until a second shape joined it and the two shapes started circling above the float.

She realized that the shapes were large black birds, and, even as she watched, a third and a fourth bird joined them, seeming to hang, wings spread, in the blue sky, flying in slow circles directly overhead.

More and more birds came, and soon there was an entire flock of rooks above the float. Martina continued to dance, but she was distracted by the strange behaviour of the birds. *What on earth are they doing up there?* she wondered. *They seem to be deliberately keeping pace with the float, almost as if they're watching our progress.*

And as if that wasn't disturbing enough, Martina noticed that dark clouds were gradually eating up the western sky. The weather forecast had been for sunshine all day, so what was bringing the rain-clouds?

'I will bring darkness to the land!' boomed a deep and extremely loud voice.

Martina jumped and turned to see where the voice had come from. She saw that Adam had climbed up on to the roof of the lorry's cab. He was standing there, arms outstretched, his cloak fanning out behind him. *Oh, no, he'll get the whole thing stopped!* Martina thought furiously. It was dangerous on the roof of the cab and Adam certainly wasn't meant to be there. He was taking things too far again. Martina hoped that Rob wouldn't see.

Adam lifted his arms to the western sky and seemed to beckon. Even as he did so, Martina noticed the dark clouds leap forwards as if driven by a hurricane wind. In a few brief seconds, the sun was covered and the daylight dimmed.

Martina stared at Adam. He was turning slowly around on the cab roof now, his arms outstretched. All the priests and followers were standing around on the float below, staring up at Adam as if they didn't know what to do next. Nothing even remotely like this had been rehearsed. But even though she knew he shouldn't be doing it, Martina had to admit that Adam's performance was impressive.

'See how I blot out the sun!' Adam boomed. 'I am God of Death. All must bow to me!'

This is getting too weird. How is he doing that voice? Martina wondered. *It's so loud and deep! Could he have a hidden microphone under the mask?* She figured that must be it – he was miked up. But in that case, where was the amplifier? The voice seemed to be coming directly from Adam's mouth – or, the mouth of the mask, anyway – but that was impossible . . .

And then, as if things weren't strange enough already, Martina heard the raucous cawing of the rooks and looked up to see them hurtling down towards Adam in a flurry of black wings. The rooks wheeled around him, cawing constantly, and a puzzled hush settled over the watching crowd.

Bewildered, Martina looked up at Sam, who was perched high on his golden throne atop the pyramid. She saw that he was leaning stiffly forward, staring intently at Adam, his lips moving, his hands gripping the arms of his chair. She waved to him, trying to get his attention, but he didn't seem to notice.

'I call down the storm upon you!' boomed the impossible voice from behind Adam's mask.

Martina felt something cold and wet touch her hand, and then, as if by some impossible magic, a flurry of wind-driven rain struck the float! Icy rain fell in torrents, billowing along the street and drenching the crowds. The parade came to a grinding halt as everyone dived for cover.

Martina cowered in the shelter of the pyramid and peered up at Adam. Somehow he remained unaffected by the storm, and was still standing on the roof of the cab, his arms outstretched and his cloak snapping and cracking in the wind. Rooks now perched on his arms and shoulders and crowded around his feet.

Crazy! He's gone totally crazy! Martina thought. *And so has the local wildlife!*

And then the storm wind grew even stronger, howling along the street like a banshee, ripping pieces off the floats and blowing people to the ground.

Martina staggered as the blast of freezing air struck her. She fell back against the pyramid, clutching it to save herself from being blown right off the lorry. She felt the ribbons being torn out of her hair and her robes flapped wildly around her.

And all she could hear above the shriek of the wind and the pounding of the rain was a rhythmic thundering sound, as if somewhere a huge leather drum were being played.

'The time has come,' breathed the impossible voice, 'for the Stealing of the Breath of Life!'

Martina recognized the words: this was meant to be the spectacular finale to Ah Puch's dance – the moment when he brought death to all the people. A dramatic routine had been worked out so that when he spoke those words, everyone around him would fall to the floor and pretend to suffocate. Martina was impressed by Adam's dedication to the performance, but she feared that the terrible wind would literally sweep him off the roof of the cab. He was so caught up in his act he seemed completely unaware of the danger.

She made her way towards the back of the cab, clinging to solid parts of the storm-racked pyramid until she could reach out and grasp the narrow metal ladder that led to the cab roof. Squinting against the howling gale and the driving rain, Martina climbed up towards Adam. The rooks were all gone now. *Probably ripped away by this wind*, she thought.

'Adam!' Martina shouted. 'Come down!'

He turned towards her and Martina reached her hand up towards him.

'Take my hand!' she cried.

Adam stepped closer, and for a moment Martina thought he was going to come down, but then she looked into the macabre, grinning mask, and saw that the eyes behind it were not the clear blue eyes of Adam Dalston, but the burning red eyes of the insanely evil creature she had seen in her nightmare.

At that moment, she realized with a jolt of pure terror that the demonic thing behind the mask was no longer her friend. And as she stared up at him in horror, Martina found herself thinking back to Adam's behaviour over the past few days: his moodiness, his tantrums, his bursts of anger – all so unlike him. And she realized that it all made sense if the evil spirit of Ah Puch – awoken when Adam first put on the mask – had gradually been coming alive inside him, infecting him, turning him into something dark and dangerous.

She watched as the black-cloaked creature on the cab roof turned away and began to dance again – a jerky, spasmodic dance, like a puppet, like something that really wasn't human. And as he danced, the rain stopped and the wind fell away to nothing. And then a new sound filled her ears – the soft, rushing noise of waves on a beach. The air seemed to spin around Martina, as if the float she was on stood at the heart of an invisible tornado.

Martina felt as if the air was being ever so slowly sucked out of her lungs. And as she tried to breathe in new oxygen, the air around her felt thin and weak. Ah Puch was stealing the breath of life. The God of Death was going to kill them all!

I have to stop this, Martina thought. She dragged

herself up on to the top of the cab, her head pounding and her chest beginning to ache. Below her, she could see people falling to the ground, choking and gasping for air.

She dragged herself towards Adam and snatched at the mask. Maybe if she got the mask off, the madness would stop. She tried not to think about the horrors that might be revealed if she did manage to pull it away.

Adam fought her. 'Get away from me,' he howled as they struggled, and this time it was his own voice that she heard. 'I have to do this!'

'No!' Martina panted, the pain growing in her chest as she tried to breathe in the vacuum that the Death God was creating. 'No, you *don't* have to!' And as she slid to the floor, she managed to tear the mask loose.

Adam fell to his knees, his face burning red and running with sweat. Martina looked into Adam's face and saw with relief that it was his *own* face, not that of a monster any more. And as she watched, the red light faded from his eyes and they became their normal blue again.

It was over.

But then Adam's hands came up to his throat and he too started gasping for air. His eyes met hers, and now Martina could see that they were filled with a terrible fear. 'It wasn't me . . .' he choked.

'I know,' she gasped. 'The mask . . .'

But Adam shook his head. 'No,' he croaked. *'Him!'* and he pointed a trembling finger over Martina's shoulder.

Her strength was failing now, but Martina turned to look where Adam had indicated, and she saw that he was pointing straight at Sam.

Sam was still on top of the pyramid, but he was standing up now. His golden robes were gone, and he was swathed in a long black cloak just like Adam's costume. He stared at Martina with a terrifying red light in his eyes, and even as Martina gazed dizzily up at him, Sam spread his arms and leaped from the top of the pyramid.

'No!' she screamed. But Sam didn't go crashing down on to the back of the lorry; he swooped through the air towards them like a great black bird and landed easily on top of the cab, his eyes burning feverishly, his mouth twisted in a cold, cruel smile.

Martina noticed that the plaster was gone from Sam's forehead, and the wound revealed was now so dark that it looked black against his pale skin.

It was in the shape of a flying bird.

Martina could hear Adam whimpering with fear and pain. She could see her other friends choking all around her. And she knew then that the true cause of all this horror and death wasn't Adam – it had never been Adam – it was *Sam*.

He was the one possessed by Ah Puch, God of Death – when he'd got the splinter from the mask on that first night. She remembered seeing Sam and Adam in the hallway at the club the morning after Sam had got the mask, and she remembered noticing how Sam had been the one doing all the talking while Adam had listened so patiently. Now she came to think of it, she could see that, all along, Sam had been controlling Adam like a puppet. When he'd told Adam to do something, Adam had obeyed.

But the realization had come too late.

Sam reached down and tore the mask out of Martina's hands. As she watched, he put the mask up to his face – and then took his hands away. He hadn't done up the strap, but the hideous mask stayed put, as if seared on to the flesh of his face. And then the mouth of the mask began to move.

'Hail to thee, Lady Rainbow,' declared a deep voice of infinite menace. 'Behold! I am free again!' The Mayan God of Death that had once been Sam spread his arms wide and threw back his head to let out a dreadful, triumphant laugh.

Martina's chest burned as she felt the last few breaths of life being sucked from her lungs. A wave of dizziness numbed her mind.

'And now, I have much work to do,' boomed the voice. 'For I am Ah Puch, and I bring death.'

Terrify yourself with more books from Nick Shadow's
Midnight Library

Vol. I: *Voices*

Kate knows that something is wrong when she starts hearing voices in her head. But she doesn't know what the voices mean, or what terror they will lead her to . . .

Vol. II: *Blood and Sand*

John and Sarah are on the most boring seaside holiday of their lives. And when they come up against the sinister Sandman, they really begin to wish they'd stayed at home . . .

Vol. III: *End Game*

Simon is a computer addict. When he's sent a mysterious new game, the lines between virtual reality and real life become terrifyingly blurred . . .

Terrify yourself with more books from Nick Shadow's
Midnight Library

Vol. IV: *The Cat Lady*
Chloe never quite believed her friend's stories about the Cat Lady. But when a dare goes horribly wrong, she finds out that the truth is more terrifying than anyone had ever imagined . . .

Vol. V: *Liar*
Lauren is shy. She just wants a friend, and she's so lonely she even imagined herself one. But she soon realizes she'd created a monster. A monster called Jennifer . . .

Vol. VI: *Shut your Mouth*
Louise and her mates love to get their sweets from Mr Webster's old-fashioned shop, but when their plan to get some of the new 'Special Delights' goes wrong, could they have bitten off more than they can chew?

Terrify yourself with more books from Nick Shadow's
Midnight Library

Vol. VII: *I Can See You*

Michael didn't want to move out of the city in the first place. And wandering round the countryside in the dark really isn't his idea of fun – particularly when he finds out how dangerous the dark can be . . .

Vol. VIII: *The Catch*

David and Adam aren't too worried when they get lost on the open sea. But when they discover an abandoned boat in the fog, things start to turn nasty. Who – or *what* – lies in wait beyond the waves . . . ?

Vol. IX: *The Whisperer*

Rachael has always wanted to be a journalist, so writing for the student paper is a perfect opportunity. But then her column begins to write itself, and soon no subject is safe . . .